MW00487395

A Continent Between Us

By

Kathleen Box

Copyright © 2018 Kathleen Box. All rights reserved.

Book cover designed by Erika Alyana,
(erika.alyana@gmail.com).
Interior layout by booknook.biz.

ISBN 10: 0-692-07868-6
ISBN 13: 978-0-692-07868-6

This story is the real life adventures taken from my Great, Great Grandfather James Addison Bushnell's handwritten memoirs. Almost every person, place, and event in this amazing account is true. Based on his facts, I've only imagined additional thoughts, daily routines and conversations to possibly explain reasons for these recorded actions. I certainly didn't need to create another thing, for his original story is extremely lively and needing no enhancements.

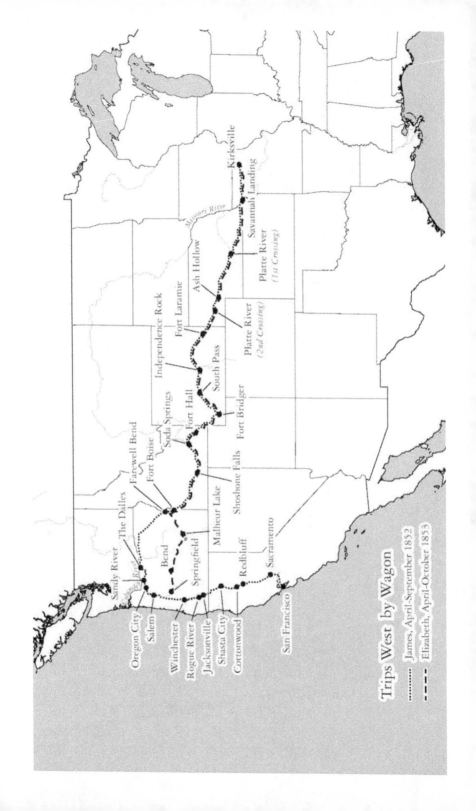

Trips West by Wagon

········· James, April-September 1852
— — — Elizabeth, April-October 1853

Kirksville
Savannah Landing
Platte River *(1st Crossing)*
Ash Hollow
Fort Laramie
Independence Rock
Platte River *(2nd Crossing)*
South Pass
Fort Bridger
Fort Hall
Soda Springs
Fort Boise
Farewell Bend
Shoshone Falls
Malheur Lake
Missouri River

The Dalles
Sandy River
Sandy River
Oregon City
Salem
Winchester
Rogue River
Jacksonville
Shasta City
Cottonwood
San Francisco
Bend
Springfield
Redbluff
Sacramento

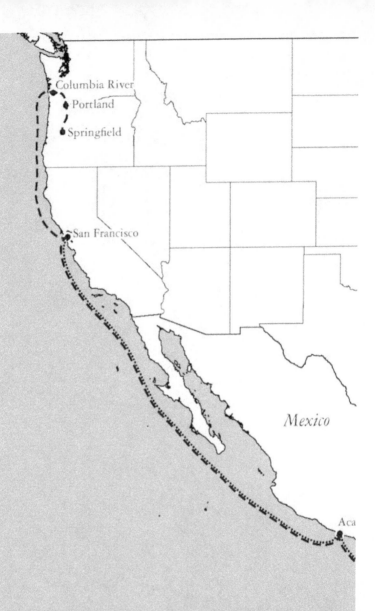

Columbia River

Portland

Springfield

San Francisco

Mexico

Aca

James' Journeys, East and West

··········· Travelling East, June 1853
‒ ‒ ‒ Travelling West, August 1853

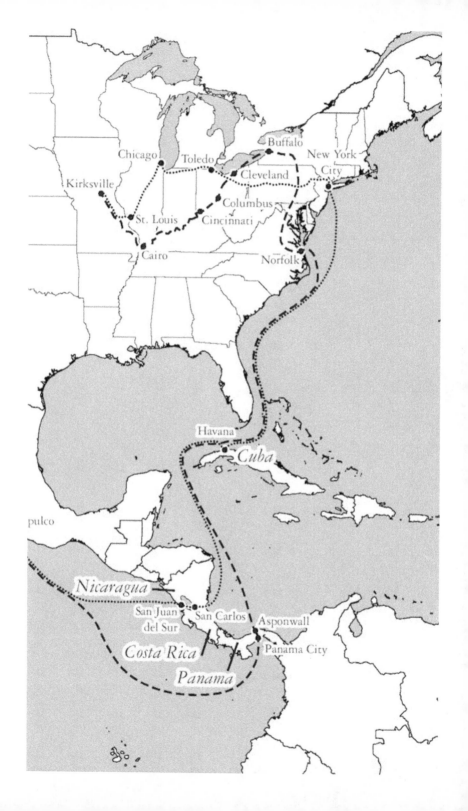

I dedicate this book, after generations of family oral accounts based on the original journal, to my dear father, Elvan McClure Pitney. Dad just recently passed away. His middle name came from one of the wagon train captains in this story. Dad was born and raised on the original family homestead near Junction City, Oregon. He lived 93 wonderful years following in the footsteps of many brave pioneers who traveled out west. Leaving what they knew and loved to start afresh in a better place, is how I think of you now, Dad.

Chapter 1

James

As he carefully made his way down the wide, muddy path some Kirksville locals called a road, young James Bushnell silently lamented over the amount of debt he was about to incur at the Farmers' Co-op. Glum feelings shadowed his calculations of the escalating winter bills acquired by his young family, his dozen or so livestock, and their eighty-acre Missouri farm. With his burdened mind and anxious stomach churning, he wondered how many more severe winters followed by meager growing seasons he and Elizabeth could survive.

James was still mentally deep in his money problems when his muddy, worn boots were suddenly stopped short by a man standing right in his path. James lifted his head to confront the tall, obnoxious figure blocking his way. Instead of a grumpy confrontation, though, he weakly choked out, "Tim?"

Tim Halsted slapped his shorter friend on the back, and his familiar grin and hearty grasp caused a warm rush to flood all over James. Seeing this old friend standing right there after more than a year sent surprising relief rolling through him like sun breaks through dark clouds.

"What are you doing here? When did you get here?" James blurted out.

Tim's quick response shot through him like a bullet, severing his life into two parts from that moment on. "Just came in today, and I'm looking for you. I'm wanting to take you off to the Oregon Territory with me. I know there's gold out there for us, James!"

Fields of gold out in the Oregon Territory? James thought. Those grand claims was enough for daring and adventurous Tim Halsted to leave Missouri. Now, Tim passionately wanted James to go with him, and as soon as possible.

Whoever heard of chunks of gold lying on the ground just waiting to be loaded up? Not twenty-five-year-old James Bushnell, that's for sure. If those pamphlets Tim had shown him could be trusted, then as they said, "Any man strong enough to get out west would be rich in no time."

James rubbed his firm jaw as he continued on to the co-op. Tim's beseeching him to partner up definitely had some appeal. James's subsistence farming of corn, oats, wheat, and vegetables had become a struggle after three harsh, long winters in a row. Without a doubt, he and Elizabeth had money troubles. They were in debt for their past two months' worth of supplies from the co-op, and he was just about to acquire another month's worth. That fact irritated him the way he imagined a burning ulcer would bother other folks.

Presently, his greatest ambition was just getting his stock, his wife, and their baby Charles fed through the next month. Now Tim had presented him with a whole new option. James reminisced as he paused on the steps of the Kirksville Co-op.

Tim Halsted was a hard worker, and he was taller and leaner than James. He was also a true friend. Five years before, they'd headed away from home together looking for work. They'd ended up along the great Mississippi making barrels on the wharf at Hannibal. James had relished the change of scenery from the family farm and its daily chores. Also, it helped that he'd quickly learned his new job. His deceased father had been a cooper once and had taught James some about making the barrels. When they weren't working, Tim and James had wandered all through that riverside town of Hannibal. That trip had become a turning point in James's life in many ways.

Within his first week in Hannibal, James visited the town's library. He started by skimming through books about different crops growing in other regions nearby and then moved on to reading about crops in other countries. He found that reading about other countries was fascinating to him, and he started dreaming about getting to a few of those places one day. The Mississippi River intrigued him too, and that interest created a desire to learn about all the big rivers in the world. He tried to memorize the names and locations of the rivers of North and South America.

The wizened librarian, Mr. Steed, often visited with James at the checkout desk. He seemed to enjoy suggesting books to the enthusiastic young newcomer. One day, he even invited James to his church, and since James was eager to make more friends, he'd agreed to meet Mr. Steed there.

Back then, Tim was more satisfied with wharf life and less interested than James in making any more friends. Tim preferred to talk, drink, and relax with the other single men they worked with. He went to the library a few times with James, but taking a book with him once or twice a month was good enough. James grew to understand that spending much more time indoors was of little appeal to Tim.

Tim also let James know he wasn't interested in church. "I might go on an occasional rainy Sunday, but don't plan on me, James," he said.

James accepted that about his friend and went alone. That first time visiting Mr. Steed's church, he enjoyed the friendliness of the people as well as the singing and preaching. To top off the good church service, he was invited to dinner by Mrs. Steed. Looking back, James remembered it was her cooking and the pleasant conversation with both the librarian and his friendly wife that'd made James so very comfortable. After dinner—and an hour more of learning about the Steeds' four grown children—James excused himself from the pretty stone-and-board house. He found Tim relaxing along the wharf with a few other men and joined them.

James went back to the church alone the next Sunday too. That had proved to be a day he'd never forget.

Now walking through the two wide aisles of the Co-op, he was distracted from his sweet memories of Hannibal life. He needed to concentrate on the list of items Elizabeth had put in his pocket while saying goodbye that morning. He gave the clerk standing behind the counter, matronly Mabel Myers, the barrel of oats he'd brought in to sell. Then he quickly found and bought what Elizabeth had asked for, not daring to look at anything else, avoiding temptation. Back at the counter with their necessities, Mrs. Myers quietly added up his costs and deducted his due for the oats. James frowned when she mentioned adding his small bill to their account, so Mabel smiled at him kindly and didn't say anything more to make James feel worse. Instead, she cheerfully visited with him about the local news and answered a few questions.

Glumly walking out of the Co-op, he went back to remembering those happy river days as he packed the saddlebag, untied his horse, and got in the saddle. He'd gone back to Steed's church that second Sunday and had listened carefully. He recalled sincerely and personally responding to the preacher's intelligent and clear Bible message. He'd left church that day with an inner joy and peace that still amazed him five years later.

Turning toward home, he thought about Tim back in those days too. From that first day in church, James had looked forward to the pastor's weekly preaching, and he'd also enjoyed that community of new friends. He'd tried again to get Tim interested in both the church and his new friends, but Tim seemed to think church was good for James but not so much for himself. It still bothered James some even now that Tim hadn't gone along with him in his new faith journey, but they didn't argue about it. They'd remained friends just the same.

Back then, James was as happy as he'd ever been. Some of that happiness was also due to a pretty young Elizabeth Atkins, who'd started coming to the church. Within their first conversation, Elizabeth had told him that her family owned a Virginia plantation, but she was staying with her aunt and uncle who resided in Hannibal. Her Aunt Emily had suffered a bout of typhoid fever but was on the road to recovery. Still, the doctor had advised Emily and her husband, Andrew, to find some help with their three little children through the coldest months of the year, so Elizabeth was spending that winter assisting her aunt.

Plodding his mare along the muddy lane out of town, James smiled as he thought about that one day after church when he'd invited Elizabeth to accompany him on his next library visit. He'd been initially shocked that she'd accepted his invitation.

He seriously wondered if she'd just been that bored and lonely back then. Given that they'd had such different upbringings, he'd doubted there was anything she'd like about him. His musing made him chuckle aloud, and his confused horse raised her ears. However, he and Elizabeth had gone to the library together that week. One trip together turned into two and then into regular weekly trips. Soon their Sunday visits at church included afternoon walks along the Mississippi. Following not long after had been dinner invitations from her aunt and uncle.

That fall and the next winter of 1847 had flown by in such a pleasant routine that James was stunned when Elizabeth started talking about returning home to Virginia in May. Even knowing the time was coming, he'd effectively denied all thoughts of her departure. Soon enough, though, Mr. and Mrs. Atkins came to visit in Hannibal before taking Elizabeth back home. James had been very nervous to meet them, but he was greeted so warmly that his fears quickly died. Apparently, Aunt Emily had sent them many complimentary words about him, for which he was deeply grateful. After the Atkins' three-day visit, James felt accepted by all.

He was encouraged that maybe he and Elizabeth could have a future together in Kirksville. He spoke these thoughts in private to Elizabeth. She was warmly responsive to his intentions. He'd surprised her when he insisted she go back home to Virginia and consider all she would be leaving behind if she married him. Tearfully, she had returned home, but they kept in touch by writing often, sometimes daily.

James kept his horse moving slowly through the winter fog. He had plenty of time to summon up his old memories. James and Tim had spent the next year working on the wharf, until they felt they'd each saved up enough to make it on their own.

After a year's absence, James was amazed that Elizabeth, back in Virginia, had refused other suitors and continued their relationship. He couldn't believe she still loved him.

The two young men returned to Missouri together. James bought eighty acres of farmland in central Adair County, and Tim bought a small livery in the north county. They kept in touch as often as they could, separated as they were by fifty miles. James built a small, cozy home on his farmland. It was only then he felt he could ask Elizabeth to marry him. A March trip to the Atkins plantation followed, and the marriage was approved by her father. They were married in April 1848 in her parents' Virginia church.

James knew only God could have caused such a strong and beautiful woman to marry him. Everyone in his part of Adair County realized what risks Elizabeth had taken when she'd married him. For as long as he could remember, his parents had kept moving their family farther west every few years to find better farmland. As a result, the Bushnells never settled very long in any one place. However, Elizabeth's roots were in an established, family-owned plantation, greater than most all the farms here in Missouri.

Initially, back in Hannibal, he'd been attracted to Elizabeth's beauty and her courage to leave her home in order to help others. As she'd accompanied him on those library trips, he learned that she, too, had a spirit for adventure; she enjoyed reading and dreaming of other lands. Bravely, and probably foolishly in love, they began dreaming of a different life they could have together. Elizabeth told him she longed to get away from the sameness of her Virginia setting as, except for Hannibal, it was the only place she'd ever lived. In response, he'd shared his dreams of getting to see more than Adair County and

Hannibal, Missouri. Now, neither he nor Elizabeth had seen a library since he'd moved them to Kirksville. Elizabeth had kept up her adventurous spirit and was most always optimistic. She'd proved to be the hard worker needed in this farm life.

Studying the fog ahead of his mare, it made him sigh aloud to think about how stuck he felt now after just three years of farming here. He mused over her spirit of adventure and optimism now as he was about to tell her what Tim had boldly proposed today. He turned his rusty mare left at the branch running toward their home.

He still had about another mile on this lane to contemplate Tim's invitation. James recalled, even way back working on the wharf, overhearing tales about the Oregon Territory from some loud passengers and some even louder boat captains. Those men had boasted about all the wealth to be had out west. Most bragging was about the fertile land, the climate, and the gold to be found. Now, three years later, Tim was confidently claiming they should both go grab that gold from the Oregon or California hills. Tim had no doubts whatsoever.

Actually, James's own older brother, William, had believed those claims too and had taken off headed west. Sadly, a year later, no one here at home knew anything about William now. His only letter had been sent when he'd reached Oregon City, stating only that he'd arrived safely. No more news had come since then, which kept them all wondering and praying often about William.

James knew that one huge difference between himself, William, and Tim was that he was responsible for a wife and child. Should he even listen to the single and carefree Tim Halsted anymore? Dare he even tell Elizabeth about Tim's proposal, let alone admit that he was thinking about leaving her and their baby for quite a spell? He decided he needed to stop and pray for God's guidance before he got too carried away with all these thoughts.

Chapter 2

As James rode his rust-colored horse closer toward home, he prayed about this risky move to leave for the west with high hopes of coming back with gold. It could be the jump start he and Elizabeth needed. Elizabeth certainly realized the many doubts he'd experienced lately about their future. During this terrible winter and spring of 1852, he'd worried aloud plenty about the farm. They needed more land and better crops for their growing family's needs. Still, to his amazement, Elizabeth never acted as bothered by their lack of money. She always appeared to love their simple life together, and he hoped she really did. He knew from the Scriptures and their common faith that security wasn't found in anything money or possessions could provide. He desperately hoped Elizabeth could keep remembering that now in these very lean years. He hoped he could too! Still, even deeply and happily in love, neither of them could deny that their farm was barely making them a living.

He desired so much more for all of them—more than he could foresee here on his small farm. The surrounding larger farms were also struggling now. James pondered all that this western venture could mean for them as his mare moved them both carefully along the rutted, muddy path.

James knew Tim was eager to join the throngs of others setting out west this spring. It sounded like hundreds were crossing the continent for the promises of gold and abundant free land. He rubbed his chin again and massaged his right temple. Years ago, that Hannibal trip with Tim had been a big gamble, and it had turned out profitably. Just like now, that trip had happened only after Tim's insistent urging, and it had turned out just like Tim had hoped. Taking chances together might just be what really worked for the two men. But how was Elizabeth going to respond to this fanatical new idea? She'd only met Tim once, briefly, on their wedding day. She really didn't have much reason to trust the man.

James prayed, *Could I dare take this big step in the hopes of providing better for Elizabeth and baby Charles?*

Thinking of his family again made him realize that Elizabeth would be waiting for him and the supplies he'd purchased at the Co-op. She'd looked pretty glum when he'd left this morning. Little Charles had been fighting a chest cold, and it worried Elizabeth to take him out in the dampness, so she'd been forced to stay home a lot lately. James's mother and two brothers lived just a few miles away from his farm, and he appreciated that they were close. However, it was still always a challenge for Elizabeth and him to get away from their own farm chores long enough to get over there and visit. Sundays used to be their best day for visiting his family, but now with little Charles's sleeping schedule or any health concerns, they couldn't even count on regular Sundays.

Even though she was a devoted homemaker and mother, he knew Elizabeth felt confined. She'd be anxious for him to get back and tell her any news he'd heard around town. He understood and sympathized, so he tried to hurry the mare a little more.

As he guided the mare between his stone field markers, he was thinking of Elizabeth affectionately. And that's when his inner voice started lecturing him. *You should just settle down and listen to good reason. Keep working your farm like everyone else around here. Hope for a better year with next year's crops. You have a great wife and darling baby and are blessed with good health.*

Just then he saw the smoking chimney he and Elizabeth had built together by hauling the rocks from along their creek. He hurried his mare toward the small timbered home.

Chapter 3

Elizabeth

What was taking James so long today at the co-op? She'd been very much looking forward to their regular trip to town together. They went twice a month, and she was always eager to pick up the town news as well as any letters from her family. She was also anxious to hear how Jane's newest pregnancy was coming along. Elizabeth tried to always visit her town friend, especially since Jane had been so weak and nauseated at their last visit.

Jane was the one new friend in Adair County whom Elizabeth had a few things in common with—like the beginnings of marriages and their first pregnancies. They'd also anticipated sharing new motherhood together. Then, sadly, Jane had lost her baby in childbirth last spring. Elizabeth remembered how dear Jane's experience had badly frightened her about her own pregnancy back then. She needn't have worried, though, as James and she had a healthy baby boy born that April. The joy of her heart now was that baby, Charles Alva!

Elizabeth was so very thrilled that Jane was pregnant again. With all the nausea and initial weariness hopefully passed, Jane should be getting excited now for the upcoming birth. They lived too far apart to see each other more than once or twice a month, and Elizabeth realized with strong yearnings that they were long overdue for a visit.

Elizabeth knew that being heavy with pregnancy was still easier in many ways than the busy work of a new baby. She used to be able to get out more to visit family and friends, go into town to gather news, and get to the community church service. Now she'd be content to just have a chance to see Jane, and even that would have to wait until Charles was over his runny nose and cough. She started daydreaming about how she could bundle up her baby and take the wagon by herself over to Jane and Tom's house. She felt pretty confident she could do that much alone, as James probably wouldn't have time. Then, Jane and she could have their own visit and catch up nicely without the men around. They needed each other at times like this, when their young husbands worked so hard and came in so tired.

Thinking of her hardworking, young husband made her wonder again what was keeping him so long. She crossed the room to look out their one front window again. She held her long, straight hair off her shoulder with one hand and with her other hand pushed the curtain away. Peering into the twilight, she was startled by a bang and then wailing from behind her. She turned to see that little Charles had crawled upon her tri-legged stool, apparently lost his balance, and was now lying on his back. The stool was usually sitting out, as she had to use it for reaching the top shelf of her kitchen hutch. Her sister had given them the hutch as a wedding present, and Elizabeth kept her few precious dishes and other breakables in that special piece of furniture. She'd soon be having to put the stool out of the reach of her young explorer. That thought frustrated her, since she was just too short for too many things. Being short was a challenge on the farm, inside and out.

She quickly picked up the howling little guy, who was more alarmed at the noisy clatter he'd made than at any real harm done to himself. With the crying little tot in her arms, she was surprised to hear the door burst open. James blew in with the cold.

"Hello, my noisy family!" He greeted Elizabeth with his big smile, a quick hug and kiss, and then took Charles into his arms. "Let me see what will help this little man." Elizabeth gave the baby over to his dad and watched with loving relief as Charles Alva quickly calmed down. As usual, baby Charles responded well to his father's attentions.

Soon James was pacing the room with Charles and in mock seriousness discussing the co-op's prices of corn and hay. He told the baby, "I barely got over three dollars for that five-pound bag of oats I took in to sell. I remember when I bought those oats for less than a dollar per pound. It's a bad winter for everyone around here, not just us." He made eye contact with Elizabeth at this point. Turning his handsome but grim face back to little Charles, he continued, "I'm happy to bring home a five-pound bag of potatoes, a bunch of wrinkled old carrots, smelly onions, and the flour your mom needed. However, it was sure hard to turn down the ham, beef, and other delicacies I was hoping to get in exchange for all those oats! I was drool-ing over the thought of fresh meat and dreaming up how I could trade a baby boy for some decent food. Then I remem-bered I could just eat his tummy—like this!" James then did his usual hungry bear imitation, growling, "I'm going to get you!" and burying his face under Charles's little cotton shirt.

It made Elizabeth laugh along with the baby. *At least some pleasures in life are free,* she thought.

All of a sudden, James stopped his nonsense and with a grin said to her, "Of course, there was other news in town." She couldn't help but giggle and clap as she watched him pull a somewhat wrinkled envelope from his wool vest. Grinning with satisfaction at her delight, James held it out to her.

She grabbed it from his hand and said, "Oh, thank you. Thank you!" She sat down on the kitchen stool with her letter.

"Certainly! Hopefully that holds more promising news than the prices at the Co-op."

He juggled and swayed with Charles as she carefully opened the envelope so as not to damage one word inside. Then turning aside, she entered her own private world and silently read the words her mother sent from Virginia. News from home always affected her two ways: some homesickness coupled with relief to be away from all the tangles of her large family relationships.

"Sounds like the plantation survived this harsh winter with few real losses so far," Elizabeth said aloud to James as she scanned the words a second time. "Emily had some serious swollen glands a few weeks back, but she's better now. Pa's still thinking of selling off some of his back fields so he can slow down and maybe take Mother to New York or Boston for their anniversary. Henry's children and Lizzie all sound about the same. I think Lizzie is still upset at all the attention Henry's kids get. She was so used to being the center of attention for seventeen years. I hope she can get past this jealousy. It sure makes it hard for Mother. Mother should be able to enjoy her grandkids without feeling guilty!

"Also, it sounds like the school board meetings have taken

more time than Father thought. Sounds likes he kind of likes that responsibility, though. 'Finds it interesting,' it says here."

James responded, "Well, that's a relief to know that at least they have suffered little this winter. I know you wish you could go visit them and show off little Charles. Henry's children need to share their grandparents. Right, Charles?" he said as he jiggled the little boy some more. The baby laughed at his dad's voice, which made both parents laugh.

"Maybe they'd come see us this spring?" Elizabeth said wishfully.

Instead of answering and getting any hopes up, James didn't reply.

"Are you ready for supper now, James? It's been done for over an hour. Really, what took you so long at the Co-op?" She got busy as she asked, starting to set their plates on the small table they used for meals—as well as everything else. She looked up just in time to see his face change to sudden seriousness and his cheerful antics with the baby turn to a slower, more methodical process of tying Charles into his chair at the table.

"I ran into more people than I imagined. It was too good of a chance to catch up with news from other parts of the country. I heard a lot of talk about the government giving out free land in the west. It's free for anyone who'll head out to the Oregon Territory and claim it. Ted Williams heard they're giving 360 acres per married couple. Can you believe that? That's more than I hope to ever own here as long as we live.

"Many folks in Springfield are selling their farms now. Then they buy wagons and the oxen to pull them. They say that oxen do better grazing off the land and don't need as much grain packed along as do horses. Also, oxen end up being stronger for the long haul but not as fast, of course. Ted's seriously thinking of joining up with his cousin and a wagon train too."

He abruptly stopped talking when he saw that supper was served, setting right in front of him, and Elizabeth was waiting on him to say Grace. They bowed their heads and held hands as he thanked God for His love and for their food.

Before he could start again and bring up Tim's surprising visit, she changed the subject. "So what did you find out about Jane and Tom? I'm wondering about her pregnancy. Did you hear any word about her?"

He slowly scooped his potatoes onto his plate without answering her right away. Before he could talk of any more grand dreams of moving west, and them with a young baby, she was diverting him back to reality. Her mind was still on babies and family life.

"Mabel, in the co-op, said Jane was doing fine and just waiting her time now. I didn't ask any more, as that's what we wanted to hear, right? We'll assume she's going to continue being healthy and deliver a big, healthy baby in a few weeks." James stopped to take a bite and chew.

Elizabeth nodded and smiled at his reassuring words. As she gave the baby a small piece of bread to gum, James started talking in a more serious voice. "My biggest news is that I ran into Tim Halsted, as he came looking for me today. He is ready to take off to the west with plans to mine gold and come back wealthy. He's convinced that it's smarter to get to the Oregon Territory than slave away here while others go get the gold ahead of him. He's a hard worker and he's read up on the reports and all that it takes." He paused to take another bite and let that news sink in.

When Elizabeth remained quiet, James went on, "He thinks

I could get rich along with him and come back here and buy some better land. Or, as Ted Williams says, I could get us 360 acres of prime farmland in Oregon, and we could settle out there. I just can hardly believe the land would be free. I know it would take a lot of work, but I'm not afraid of hard work. It's almost too good to be true. Gold and free land to choose from, or get both on the same trip!"

Finally, Elizabeth said, "Is that the reason Tim came to Kirksville? To find you and convince you to go? Doesn't he remember you're married and have a baby now? I don't know why he'd think we could pack up and leave just like that! We've family here, and the only family that's gone out west, your brother, no one has heard from since."

"I think we should think about it, Elizabeth," James countered. "Our future here is not looking promising, as you know. I want better for you and Charles. I don't like the debts we've had to get into just to live and survive."

They finished the rest of the meal in silence.

Chapter 4

James

In the spring of 1852, two weeks after Tim asked James to come with him, the two men were at the Missouri River crossing called Savannah Landing. James was quite surprised at the immense crowd gathered and camped here. In fact, the crowd of emigrants was so huge that James and Tim had both halted on the hillcrest, livestock and all, and stared over the scene before them.

James said, "It's truly amazing that so many others made such a big decision, as we did, to travel west. I am sure surprised! And I hope there's enough gold out there for all of us."

After taking it all in, Tim moved first and carefully urged their oxen down the sloping hillside toward the huge group below. Following, James felt better about his decision as he rode his mare down into that mass of travelers. Seeing so many others here confirmed that he must not be crazy to leave home. Apparently many others were thinking like him. Nevertheless, it had been a very difficult decision to make, and James still wasn't sure if Elizabeth entirely understood. Being able to leave

Charles and her in the care of his mother and brothers, though, had helped ease his decision to venture out west.

His brothers had been supportive of James taking off for the gold mines of California. He'd changed his aim toward the California gold mines, rather than head for Oregon's free farmland. Just as he'd expected though, his mother had voiced strong concern over him leaving Elizabeth and the baby. However, having been married to his pa, his mother knew that Bushnell men had an itch to keep searching for a better life wherever they could. His pa had often moved the whole family farther west in search of better land too. From New York to Pennsylvania to Ohio to Missouri, they'd moved in just James' childhood. Mother seemed to finally believe James's desire was really about bettering his family's future. Then, she quickly agreed to support Elizabeth and baby Charles as much as she could and so did his two younger brothers, Jason and Cory. James knew he could trust them all to help out Elizabeth. Still, no denying it—the decision hadn't been easy to make.

Now, on this their first step of the journey, James observed that crossing over from the south to the north bank of the Missouri was going to be a challenge. Even before that, it was going to take some patient waiting, as there was a very long line ahead of them. The two young men ended up camping on the southern edge of the huge group of wagons and off to the side of most of the herds. After tying off his horse, James helped Tim set their oxen and cows off to graze with the others. Then they each unloaded their bedding and set up a campfire spot where they could cook later. Then, after tending the horse with food and water, they took off for a walk around the edge of the large camp area. It felt good to stretch their legs.

People were friendly enough in greeting, but those closest

by had just gotten there too. Most were busy setting up camp-sites to accommodate their families and taking care of their personal stock. Few were unaccompanied men like James and Tim, who got back to their wagon spot with just enough daylight left to get cooking. After eating, their first adventurous day ended by visiting with the family groups camped closest to them. They learned a few names and heard more glorious speculations from the men nearest them about the rewards up ahead on their journey.

It was a noisy night spent with all the sounds of animals and so many families camped around them. James tossed and turned on his bed on the ground, finding it very hard to get com-fortable. He regretted not setting his bedding in the wagon and vowed he sure would do it the next night.

The next day, by obvious necessity, the large group was divided into many smaller groups, or "companies," by a couple of older men who introduced themselves.

Tim had talked his friend Elik Nesbit into joining them at this landing spot too. Elik found them among the throngs of those waiting on the riverbank, and the three young men now stuck together in their assigned group. Elik added his horse and bedding to their campsite and settled in. He had journeyed a day and night from northern Missouri to get there, so he gladly joined in the wait for their company's turn.

James had met Elik on the wharf back in Hannibal and now enjoyed getting caught up with the other man's news. Elik had returned to Adair County soon after James himself had left Hannibal, and more recently he'd worked for Tim at the livery stable.

Elik said, "Over the past three years, I spent most of my earnings from the wharf job just trying to get my own farm started. Mostly frustrated all three years, I finally just turned my farm over to my younger brother. Now, I'm hoping to get something better out west or start some new kind of adventure. I don't care only about farming, and there may be something more prosperous-looking for me to do out there. And to tell you the truth, James, I am not sure about heading all the way south to California with you two. I'll decide later on, because I figure I've got plenty of time on the trail ahead to think about my destination."

James agreed, saying, "I think that's going to be an interesting way for you to decide, all right."

Camping and waiting there at the landing, James had some time to start following through on his plan to take notes describing his trip, something like a journal. This would help him remember the important sights and details later. But on the banks of the Missouri, he was struck with a new idea: he could send his notes back home to Elizabeth periodically along the route. It was a better way to tell her and all the family about his travels, and she could keep them safe for him too. He knew Elizabeth would naturally share his news with the rest of the family. He'd just include some of his notes in each letter home. He got excited with this new inspiration and dug out the loose paper he'd packed away for this reason. He enthusiastically started his notes there at Savannah Landing.

On the second day of waiting, his writing time was interrupted when their group was assigned a wagon captain. Their new captain introduced himself as Mr. Wilson, and he seemed nice enough. After introductions all around, Captain Wilson gazed back at James and said, "I see you've been writing. Is it a letter back home?"

James cheerily replied and quickly explained his idea about

keeping a journal and posting it back to his wife and mother. Much to James's dismay, Wilson said, "I'm sorry to tell you that you can only expect to find two mail offices along this whole journey, and that's including one at Fort Dalles in Oregon. Keep your journal for sure, young man, but don't count on it getting to your loved ones from along the way."

This sour news ended up making James feel much worse about his decision to leave and cause this long separation from his family. He still had a few doubts about his taking off like this, but he managed to keep them to himself and to the Lord in prayer. He wasn't about to admit to anyone but God that he was already missing his family—especially not to his two single companions.

Chapter 5

Elizabeth

March 1852

Baby Charles was fussing. When Elizabeth opened her eyes, there was already a crack of daylight coming in through the wooden shutters. She turned over in bed and stretched her arms, and then she froze. She was all by herself!

James had left in their old wagon with Tim just yesterday. The promises of gold and free land everyone talked about all over their county had been too much for him to resist. After two weeks of arguing back and forth, he'd finally convinced her that if she just let him go for nine to twelve months, their family's future would be much more promising. His plan was to either return rich enough to buy better land here or take them back with him to the richness of the Oregon Territory. As she'd reluctantly listened, he reasoned it'd be worth it for him to make this trip. Additionally, he'd gone on to assure her that his two brothers and mother would help her run the farm while he was gone. It didn't take much more for her to recognize that he'd already replaced his farming hopes here in Adair County with dreams out in some new country somewhere. And she knew his new dream was strong enough for him to leave home to go after it. It had proved futile to resist his talk after a week or so. His whole family had finally accepted his departure plans, and eventually she did too.

She unfroze and sighed deeply in their bed—her bed, now. He had worn her down with all his dreams and talk. More fully awake, she wondered, by letting James go, what had she done to herself and their baby?

Well, "one day at a time," as her mother had always said, and her baby needed attention. She got up and stirred the embers first thing and added some of the small pieces of wood James had stacked up before leaving. Then she put the pot of water she'd filled up last night on the fire to heat. She'd learned that the baby's noises weren't as urgent as getting these things done first, before her arms and hands were full with her little one.

Off to her toddler she went next. She swept him up, quilt and all, for a morning hug. She greeted him and thanked God out loud for their new day. She wanted little Charles to hear her voice and her words, as he'd be learning to talk himself soon. It was important that he hear loving words as much as possible. She laid him on the table to change his diaper. She kissed his little feet, both up in the air, as she removed the wet cloth. He smiled and giggled at his mother's attention. Their delightful morning routine helped her start every day joyfully and thankfully, especially today when she needed it so much. Little Charles Alva was always such a blessing!

As a mother, she didn't comprehend how James could stand being away from their baby for nine months. As she walked with the baby to the rocking chair, she doubted she'd ever really understand that about men. Other men had left their families behind too. Settling into nursing and rocking, she mused about her future in the next few days, let alone the next nine months. She knew that James's younger brother, Jason Bushnell, was going to come by every day after his own morning chores, to check and help her as needed. She had cows, horses, and fowl to care for daily. She knew she could feed chickens and gather eggs, but she was certainly counting on Jason's help with the rest of the animals.

Jason and Cory had accepted the task of also seeding and tending her wheat and corn fields while James was gone. They would probably end up harvesting it too, depending on James's return. It was doubtful to all of them that James would make it back that quickly. Seasonally, all the small farmers gathered to help each other with their harvests, though, so her brothers-in-law would have more help then.

Also, she'd been reassured that Mother Bushnell was more than willing to help with the baby any time, and Elizabeth was really depending on that offer.

Elizabeth also knew she had an option to live with her in-laws; they'd offered more than once. However, she thought it would be easier for everybody if she stayed in her own home. She didn't want to move just because James had left home. She didn't feel in danger, and she knew the family would all be checking in with her. She certainly did plan on accepting their dinner invitations and enjoying their company. The brothers and Mother would help keep her up on the latest news from town.

"Reckon we'll get by, little one. We're just going to be forced to depend on the Lord and all the others nearby to help us out. That's not such a bad thing, really." The baby looked up into her eyes and smiled, and she felt a real peace about it all. Would she still have this peace tomorrow, she wondered.

Chapter 6

James

Savannah Landing, Missouri
April 8, 1852

Always an optimist, and regardless of Captain Wilson's discouraging news about the scant mail posts along the trail, James enthusiastically continued his notes while they camped and waited to cross the river. He described the crowds and their surroundings. Then he told Elizabeth about Elik joining them and described what he looked like:

> Elik is younger than Tim and I by two years. We all knew each other back on the Hannibal wharf. Tim kept in touch with him and acquired his help at his livery business about a year ago. He is strong enough, tall and slight of build. His hair is dark, his stubble is still sparse, and his black eyes take in his surroundings cautiously. He is not as friendly, nor as warm mannered as Tim. His character is still unproven, but traveling together for the upcoming months will give him many opportunities to demonstrate it. As he is Tim's friend, I am satisfied to take him on as a part of our little expedition of three, at least for now.

He described the river scene before him as "a very large

group spread out like a fan on the south side of the Missouri." He described the muddy, wide river and then how the ferry operator slowly took one family or two small groups across. That family's stock swam across the river at the same time their ferry crossed. Once the groups and all their stock were across—and that wasn't always easy—the ferry, a scow that had to be rowed, went back to the dock. Only then did another family get to drive carefully onto the wooden boat. James certainly wished there was another ferry or two working here in addition to this one man's. That one ferryman must be making a very decent living off of all these emigrants.

Eventually, when that was all noted on paper, James just walked around and waited like all the others until it was finally their turn to cross.

He wrote more two days later and in the days after they crossed the river.

April 10, 1852
We finally crossed by ferry. Our ferry boat was an old
wooden scow propelled by two oars. The river was wide,
and with many more rapids than my liking. Even though
I can swim, I certainly was hoping not to have to prove it.
The ferry swayed abruptly when it was first caught in the
current, and I had to steady my feet and hold on to the
rails. Surprisingly, through most of the crossing the old raft
floated smoothly along. I still felt relieved when we got
ourselves, the horses, the wagon, our teams of oxen, and
my two cows safely across. Landing on the north bank, we

reorganized with our wagon company and waited for a few other single men to get across.

Getting off the river and started down the trail took most of that day. Still, we took off late that day on the well-worn path left by all the others ahead of us. By the end of our next day, we suddenly found ourselves out of the pale man's civilization, with not a single white settler in this entire region. We know other emigrants are ahead of us, but none others to be seen that actually live here. How amazing that one river crossing could make such a difference in our surroundings. I am already in unsettled territory!

Kansas Territory
April 12, 1852
The trail leading to the land of gold was however crowded with white-topped wagons. The prairie grass had just started to grow on the bare hills of Kansas. We left civilized life behind us and turned our faces toward the setting sun. We began our long journey across the Plains in the company of many other hopeful enthusiasts.

When we reached the Kansas Territory at the end of our third day, we met hundreds more covered wagons. Most of these new wagons were families bound for Oregon, but there had to be at least fifty of us single men all seemingly bound for California. We quickly settled in with this bigger wagon train, as our group, led by Captain Wilson, was instructed to do.

Indian Agency
April 22, 1852
*The first sign of life we found after many days of traveling
was on the Indian Agency. The government agency had
built many good houses and farms enclosed with sturdy
fences here. It was comforting to see signs of civilization so
far from where we'd left our own towns and homes.*

*I can't wait to tell my little boy in person that it was
here I saw my first Indian! I'm not sure if he was Iowa,
Sauk, Fox, Kickapoo, or Potawatomi, as I learned rem-
nants of all those tribes live here along the trail here. It
happened right after we crossed Wolf Creek by way of a
toll bridge built by the local Indian tribes. I'm sure our
government agents taught them how to build this strategic
bridge and now we, and all fellow Americans, pay very
well to cross it.*

*Now, as far as our eyes could see, the road was crowd-
ed with wagons waiting to cross the bridge. Then I saw
him, an old chief, wrapped in dirty, torn blankets with a
string around his waist that formed a pocket for his coins.
He acted as the toll collector. We watched him do his job
as we sat there relaxing and waiting our turn. He did this
without speaking much English. He just grunted and held
out the bag, saying, "Five," as each emigrant passed by
him. We all easily understood we were giving him five
cents apiece to cross.*

*Finally tired of waiting there, I hollered, "Tim, I'm
going on up ahead to wait in the sunshine." Going on
some distance ahead, I alighted from my mare and climbed
up on a high rail fence and closed my eyes to rest. Soaking
up the sunshine made it easy enough to nod off. I was*

soon startled, however, by a strong smell and a strange feeling. Opening my eyes, I took in the sight of pork fat on the end of a long stick being placed beneath my nose! Turning quickly around, I was surprised by the sight of a tall Indian at the other end of that stick. Even without words, I could tell I was supposed to buy this. Not wanting to upset him, I quickly obliged. Thankfully, it was tastier than it smelled. These were my first Indians: both in the same day, but probably not my last by many more to come.

We camped here and tried to keep ourselves occupied with preparations on our wagons and supplies. It was too long of a wait for men like the three of us. We were very impatient to get going again.

Nearing Fort Kearney
May 1, 1852
We finally were able to cross the sturdy bridge and start on our way. Leaving the Indian Agency behind, our train continued on to the Platte River. This river appeared broad, muddy and mostly shallow.

After three days of travel, we heard rumors that we were just south of our first fort, Fort Kearney. Arriving there, we soon were surprised to encounter a large body of soldiers that escorted us to the newer Fort Kearney. They explained that the old Fort Kearney had been discontinued, as it was off the beaten path. Wisely, in our opinion, the newer fort had recently been built by our government and was closer to the trail. The soldiers said its purpose was to assist emigrants like us headed to California and Oregon.

Arriving there, I saw that this fort was a series of about fifteen wooden and adobe buildings outlining a four-acre parade ground.

As Tim, Elik, and I went to resupply our flour and oats, we had a pleasant surprise. "The price of oats here is better than I paid back home," I commented.

"Yep," Tim agreed. "I see what you mean. These prices are good news!"

Overhearing our comments, the clerk informed us, "The government pays us to keep the prices cheap for all folks on the wagon trains. We get our own fair price that way, and you get help supplying your journey. Those back in Washington, DC, really want to see you travelers all make it out west and settle down there. Enjoy the help while you can. Who knows how long they'll be able to keep putting money into our fort. It's been this way for three years now, and I keep wondering how much longer they can afford it."

Captain Wilson took advantage of this encouraging environment, and our train set up a wide camp and settled in for some extra days of resupplying.

Several hundred other travelers were passing through here at the same time, and all the crowds made for quite a long wait. It took several days, as the captain had predicted, to get our restocking tasks accomplished. While waiting at this camp, everyone eventually heard that all these troops were here to hold the wild Pawnee Indians in check. Rumors of this unpredictable tribe spread quickly through the train, creating a nervous feeling around our campfires. Anxious to get going on our way, we were also anxious about being well prepared before leaving that reassuring military protection.

Leaving Fort Kearney for the North Platte junction
May 8, 1852
Resupplied and ready, most of our wagon train departed, following the Platte River upstream. This route would bring us to its junction with the North Platte, according to the captain. A few families stayed behind for further rest and replenishing at Fort Kearney, with the plans of catching up.

Our group arrived two days later at the anticipated river junction with the North Platte. The whole group stopped, looked at the river crossing, and considered our options. Some of us young men and the captain were selected to scout out the best crossing place.

To me it was a mighty strange-looking river, being from one half to one mile wide and with low banks two to four feet high. The boiling water trapped in eddies was as full of muddy sand as I'd ever seen before.

Seeing how shallow it was made me feel quite brave. I called out, "Fellows, watch my back. I'm going to give it a try by foot." Making sure they'd heard me, I cautiously stepped in the water and found it not more than a foot deep. And, it was only a foot deep for the first quarter or more. So much for my bravery, I thought sheepishly.

Captain Campbell, hearing what I was doing, hollered over, "Son, watch out for quicksand!" I gulped. I had acted so brave out of my ignorance.

However, now more fully aware of the quicksand danger, I still wanted to wade across the river. Cautiously stepping out further, I found it only up to three feet deep, but mostly all loose sand on the bottom. This was a new and intriguing experience for me, and I experimented walking around some more. I was very glad to have Tim and Elik keeping a watch from the shore with their rope ready, just in case they needed to pull me out.

I carefully made it more than two-thirds across and through the deepest area. Then I turned back to the shore where I'd left from and waved to the others there. Slowly reaching the shore again without needing any assistance gave me a heady, triumphant feeling!

Then, since we were still waiting for the last group of our train to catch up, each of us traded spots, and Tim and Elik took their turns practicing the crossing. Each man took his time entering the water and getting his stance. Then carefully keeping his balance, each walked across in the sandy water. The other two or more of us were always watching and ready with the rope. Most all in our train watched our trial crossings and cheered us on our success. However, I noticed all of them were still very careful about getting near this river.

Eventually our whole wagon train was together again the next day. Then, we started our crossing of all the wagons and animals. The quicksand threat made the crossing fearful for many, but by the end of the day we had all made it safely across without the loss of any animal or wagon.

Onto the South Platte River junction
May 13, 1852
Traveling just a few miles, we came upon the junction of
the South Platte River. This crossing appeared to be a
completely different story than the last one. Here, waters
were chest high, churning swiftly along, and looked as wild
as the previous crossing had looked tame.

Captain Campbell ordered, "Stop and raise your
wagon beds, then double-team each wagon." His plan was
to use double the animal power to move each wagon
strongly through the high and rapid waters. Even before
that'd happen, though, we had to painstakingly raise each
of the wagon beds onto wooden blocks high enough to keep
the water out.

Elik groaned as he dismounted his young black
stallion. Everyone could see that all this was going to take
more time than we liked. We men knew we had it so
much easier than the families among us, though. The
families had so much more packed into their wagons, most
all of which had to be unpacked before raising the floor.
Plus, most families had their children to contend with
during this extra work. Elik strode off with our horses,
oxen, and cows to find a good grazing spot, as Tim and I
looked at each other soberly and resigned ourselves to
helping the others.

Unloading the others' wagons, I found it quite inter-
esting to see what each family had chosen to bring along.
Tim and I began giving each other questioning looks and
eventually exchanged some smiles as we worked helping
unload wagons. I assumed that each family considered their

items valuable enough to transport all the way out west. That's why we kept being surprised.

Two wagons had barrels of flour with china dishes packed inside the flour. We were told to be especially careful with those barrels. Some wagons had extra bed frames, chests of drawers, spinning wheels, fancy dish cupboards, and one even had a harpsichord; we figured most of those were probably the women's choices. Our greatest surprise was the one farmer who had managed to get a heavy iron plow inside his wagon. That was when Tim and I silently rolled our eyes at each other and suppressed any comments in fear of saying the wrong thing or even laughing aloud. Certainly there would be a black-smith somewhere out west who could've made a plow just as good as that old heavy thing. Nothing seemed very special about that plow to me, except possibly its extreme weight when we had to lift it. I sympathized with the poor woman and her two children sharing the wagon with that heavy piece, but managed to keep those thoughts to myself too.

Even as we all spent hours helping unload, it was obvious that keeping the wagons and all the goods safely dry was necessary and worthy of our efforts. It certainly proved worthwhile as soon as we watched the first wagons cross over just before dusk that day. The husband or driver usually sat upon the bench alone. Captain Wilson recom-mended it safer to keep all children inside the wagon bed. Most often we could see the wife, usually with the smallest child in her arms, peering out just behind her husband's seat.

Tim and I watched from the shore. Every time a

wagon first entered the river, it lurched suddenly as the current caught the sideboards. Several times the men would be yelling at their oxen or horses, "Go, go! Keep moving. Don't stop!" and inside the panicky children were yelling, "Stop! Stop!"

After the animals got their bearings and moved slowly along across the current, I'd still hear occasional cries coming from the younger family members huddled inside. Thus, it was a relief for everyone in each wagon, and those on the shores watching, when the stock got their footing again on the far bank of the Platte. The animals strained against the weight of wet wood and their passengers, working their load up the bank. As each wagon emerged dripping river water and reached higher ground, the crowd all cheered! Often I could see the family inside hug each other, or some just loosened their death grips.

I've never seen so many men hug their stock once they were stopped and on level ground. I completely understood it. The oxen or horses were heroes to everyone a part of this dangerous task. These procedures were all repeated for another four days.

Finally on the fourth day it was our turn to drive our own wagon and stock across the river, and Elik returned from watching the animals and joined us to help out once again. Seemingly it didn't bother him to just appear like that when it was our turn. Elik's selfish attitude here made me thankful Tim was my partner for the gold fields. I could appreciate that because earlier on, as we were riding along the trail, Elik had told me his plans were starting to form. Once we got out west he planned to depart up for the north. He wanted to explore the unknown regions

*above the Columbia and see what work he could find
there. Obviously, the allure of gold hadn't hooked him as
it had Tim and me, and now I was very glad for that. I
resented Elik's unwillingness to do more than just his part.*

*Finally when all the wagons were safely across, it
seemed miraculous that we'd had no calamities! The captain called, "We're going to stop, rejoice in the good
Lord's protection, and rest for a spell. Everyone take some
time to just be thankful and appreciate our safe crossing.
We're camping here tonight, as tomorrow some of you still
need to repack yet."*

*No one complained. Nevertheless, that rest stop seemed
not nearly long enough. Early the next morning, Captain
sent word that it was time to start the job of lowering all
remaining wet wagon beds back into position again. Then
all the items needed to be repacked into their proper places.
This took not just hours, but a good day to get each
pioneer family and their stock ready to move. I was pleased
that even Elik helped out this time. With all the men and
women busily getting ready to roll, it took two more days.
The time and work was necessary before we could start out
again, and yet I heard some grumblings from tired folks
around me.*

We all slept along the South Platte another night.

*Traveling a high ridge to Ash Hollow
May 20, 1852
Finally setting out, we slowly began ascending up to the
top of a rolling, high ridge. Traveling upon this massive
ridge, we covered miles of that tableland between the South*

and North Platte rivers. Reaching a narrow point that made a natural descent, we started downwards. We followed the sloped opening into an area marked Ash Hollow on the captain's guidebook. The riverside here was lined with many tall ash trees, but most of their undergrowth had long ago disappeared. Everywhere we looked there were traces of leftover campfires. Obviously, many other emigrants had been here before us.

Without stopping there, our train kept going further on to make our camp along the North Platte River. We soon encountered the worst mishap of our journey so far.

Ash Hollow Camp
May 25, 1852
We had just started to set up camp when terrific howling winds and torrential rains overcame us. Within the first hour, that rain turned into hailstones the size of hens' eggs. Neither I nor any of those around me had ever seen hail that huge. We didn't have much time to watch the storm, though.

Tim yelled above the din of hail and wind, "Get in the wagon, fellas!"

I watched Elik and Tim climb in, but before I followed them, I looked to grab a few single riders to come share our shelter. I called out to the first two men I saw who were out on their own.

"Harry, get in here with us. Tom, you too." Holding on for support against the wind, I walked to the end of the wagon bed. Peering from the end corners I saw another rider. "Johnny, we can squeeze you in. Get in here!"

Crawling in from the back end after these others, I turned and watched other single men scurry under the wagons nearest them. By now it seemed each family was huddled safely inside their fragile canvas tops.

Once under shelter, we quietly just stared out at the noisy phenomenon going on all around. Still astonished, some started expressing their fears.

"This wind and hail will destroy the canvas covers," Harry called out.

Another voice shouted, "We're not tied down tight enough for this wind!"

"We could get swept into the river if all this rain and the wind don't let up soon!" I recognized that voice as belonging to Elik.

"Lord," I prayed loudly, "I know you specialize in calming storms. We could really use your help right now. Make this storm subside, or keep us safe from danger in spite of it." After a few "Amens" were heard, we all sat helplessly watching what was happening outside. It took an hour for the hail to subside, turn into rain, and then finally settle into a drizzle.

All in our wagon load crawled out. Elik went to recheck our animals while Tim and I checked the tethers and re-secured the wagon's canvas top. Most of the other men were doing the same, and we marveled at the size of the hail that still lay on the ground. With that work done, we set up a small camp and settled in for the night. Trying to block out the wailing wind and any lingering worries, I covered my head, closed my eyes, and actually fell asleep.

Little did I know then that a danger greater than that storm would hit us next.

Wyoming
May 26, 1852
*Within twenty-four hours, a very virulent form of the
dreaded cholera began to spread amongst us. As soon as
the news of the sickness reached the captain, he ordered,
"Everyone boil your water!" Apparently some of our water
had been contaminated by our last river crossing. That was
easier to believe than that it was caused by poor cleanliness
in some peoples' personal use.*

*By the second day, even after the captain's orders
about boiling our water supply, many wagons had family
members weakened by severe diarrhea and vomiting. The
disease's powerful stench was overwhelming and sobering to
all who hadn't contracted it.*

*We struggled along over the next couple of weeks with
the disease striking many new wagons daily. If someone
became affected, few of those were strong enough to survive.
Death would come within twenty-four hours in most cases.
We left hundreds of our friends in unmarked graves along
our trail.*

*Many of the remaining family members walked or rode
silently along in shock or despair, as they were forced to
keep moving in such terrible grief. I remembered how hard
it'd been for my family to bury our father back on our own
land in Missouri. Here I watched these friends have to
bury their loved ones along some strange trail, knowing
they'd most likely never get back to their burial spot ever
again. To help those families dig graves as I did, and then
watch them set their dear one into that foreign ground, was
as heartbreaking as anything I'd ever seen before. We all*

were in some type of grief as our solemn wagon train crept slowly along.

I, along with my companions, Tim and Elik, were all deeply grateful for the good health we'd been given. Never again did I take my health for granted after that week when that disease struck and took so many in our wagon train.

High Plains of Wyoming
June 15, 1852
When we finally came to some wide-open plains, it was a good time for our animals to rest and graze peacefully. Captain Wilson instructed everyone to stop here for a few days, as we needed it as much as the stock did.

He spoke a warning: "The hills ahead of us are grueling and quite an ordeal to climb. Following the hills are the roughest mountain trails we've seen, and they lay just beyond here. This is a decent place to set up camp for a few days to rest ourselves and clean up."

After camps were set up, I watched as women set about doing laundry, shaking out bedding, and getting other belongings out of the wagons to air. For many of the others, they used this time to silently heal.

The Laramie River
June 18, 1852
Taking off to the north, we followed the Laramie River, which eventually joined the North Fork of the Platte again. This tall-grassy land was flat and the landscape so

similar that it could've been easy to get our directions confused if not for the river. It was dreary and hot, and increasingly boring walking mile after mile. The grasses were so tall and the ground so level that the most I could see up ahead of me was some heads of the taller adults walking alongside their dirty-white canvas tops.

This repetitive, dull scenery made coming upon another river extremely exciting to me. Approaching that river crossing, I saw a ferry boat landing. Beyond that was a fort. Hurray for civilization, again!

Fort Laramie
June 26, 1852
At the Laramie River crossing, we took our turns waiting for each wagon and family and all the stock to get across. It was tediously slow, as I'd learned to expect by now. At least the river was calm, and there were no major mishaps. Finally, it was our turn to board the ferry, and we paid six dollars for the wagon and stock. We got across without incident to our wagon then watched as our two horses and oxen made it safely across next.

Wading out of the water following after our last ox, Tim declared, "What a relief to make it to a fort again! Anyplace is going to be more interesting than those plains we just covered. It's worth the ferry money just to leave that all behind us." He and Elik had split the ferry costs with me. I fully agreed with his sentiments.

The ferry brought us across to Fort Laramie. Riding my mare up to the first of the wagons ahead, I was surprised to see another wide-open fort that was missing stockades or any walled enclosures. Instead, I could only see a long, rough, wooden two-story building with some smaller adobe brick structures scattered around. The long wooden building proved to be the barracks for the soldiers. A cheery Lieutenant Campbell welcomed the first in our train, and those up front heard him say this was the second United States fort built in the past several years.

"Folks, we are here solely to provide supplies and protect all you passing through to the west. There are provisions you'll find in those two smaller brick buildings, and there's an army doctor in that adobe building. The largest white building across that way is the officers' and soldiers' quarters, and we do ask that you leave them be. They have work to do. You're welcome to stay here as long as you'd like."

After restocking and resting but a few days here in the fort's open flat lands, Captain started our train moving again. We began the long, tedious climb into the foothills of the Rocky Mountains.

Independence Rock
July 1, 1852
Slowly working our way through the many foothills, we followed the smaller Sweetwater River and reached Independence Rock in two long days. This was a well-noted landmark in the emigrant calendar, as many other trains had reached this same camp spot about the time of the nation's Independence Day. Thus, it was given its name to commemorate the national holiday. This massive rock also served as a checkpoint on the emigrant calendar.

It was common knowledge among emigrants and their guides that any wagon train that managed to get here close to July fourth was on a good schedule. The ideal wagon train duration was four or five months from Missouri to Oregon, which promised an arrival before the winter snows started.

Knowing we were on schedule by reaching this land-mark on July first relieved all of us. A one-day holiday was declared by the captain. We celebrated the holiday, and just as importantly to us, we celebrated our timely arrival to this famous rock. Fiddles were brought out around the evening campfires, and couples began to dance. We sang as many patriotic songs as the musicians could remember and several that they couldn't. Even some of those weakened by the cholera and some of those grieving their lost loved ones joined in and clapped along or at least smiled.

The next day I inspected this landmark more care-fully. Our camp, and the pattern of many previous camps, surrounded a monstrous and almost flat rock lying close to the trail. This Independence Rock covered close to a third of a mile. Here previous travelers had carved their names along its sandstone sides and up on top. Many had left messages for friends and family they hoped were coming along after them. It was intriguing for me to read over the many scribbled notes. After walking completely around the sides, and without seeing any familiar names, I climbed up on the big dome-shaped rock to look over the rest of the messages. Taking more time than most others, after inspec-ting them I was still disappointed to see no "William Bushnell" or any other friend's or relative's name. My brother had left over a year ago. Since our family still hadn't heard from William, I was disappointed not to discover any messages from him nor even his name.

Following the Sweetwater River through the Rocky Mountains
July 3, 1852
Moving on before the fourth, our train made its next camp on the headwaters of the Sweetwater River. We'd crossed this small river several times on our journey since leaving Fort Laramie.

Waking the next morning, I found everything frozen stiff! Being it was July, we were truly caught by surprise.

The captain informed us, "We are in the southern part of the Rockies. Coming at this end of the mountains means we'll cross at South Pass. Then we leave these mountains behind us."

We made very good time, as that same day we crossed a high, bare ridge amid squalls of snow and hail—South Pass! I had to exclaim my excitement, "Just think about it, fellows. That means we'll soon be flowing west with all the rivers up ahead of us!"

Continuing across the mostly bare ground, by late afternoon we descended into the Bear River valley. Here the news spread that we were coming to another landmark called Soda Springs. When we stopped, I saw and tasted actual soda water coming up from the many underground springs there! It was reportedly good for bathing and medicinal purposes. I and all the other brave folks who *tasted it discovered its unpleasant taste, and no one could avoid its unpleasant smell.*

The captain told us we needed to keep our stock away, as the alkaline in the water was harmful to drink in large amounts. That was easier said than done, as our train camped there a couple of days. We had to keep a close watch on our stock as we let them graze daily.

Soda Springs, Idaho
July 7, 1852
In our wagon company, most folks were bound for Oregon. It was while camping at Soda Springs that many emigrants reconsidered their two options: turning toward the southern route toward California or continuing to the northwest for Oregon. Tim and I were convinced to change our plans by the Oregon enthusiasts around us. We listened to several men claiming the southern Oregon hills were just as profitable for mining and then decided to take their advice and make that our destination. So, instead of heading toward California as we'd always planned, now we parted with many of our friends and kept to the northern route. I wondered as we turned away if I'd ever see any of those traveling companions after this. It left me solemn and saddened to think not.

Along with Elik and our new friends, the Higleys and the Campbells, and with many others, we departed on the promising northern road leading toward old Fort Hall. All around us lay a beautiful country with fine grazing land as we rolled along the valley of the Snake and Portneuf Rivers. Traveling this luscious valley for the next week, all the families around our wagon relaxed. Though it wasn't too long before some were anxious to get to Fort Hall. That would be the next chance of getting more supplies since leaving Fort Laramie over two weeks ago. I heard some families were quite desperate for more supplies and some needed wagon repairs.

Fort Hall, Idaho
July 23, 1852
The grand ol' flag fluttering above the fort was a welcome sight! Fort Hall had originally been a trading post of the British Hudson's Bay Company, but now it was owned by the United States.

Upon arriving, I saw they'd built a safe and sturdy fort consisting of a large, enclosed square with high, thick adobe walls. I'd finally found the first fort on our trip with actual walls around it. This is how I had always considered a fort to look, and I felt much more protected.

Fort Hall's inner walls were lined with shops, stores, and small, one-room homes. All of these faced inwardly toward the square. Seeing a blacksmith's shop, finally emigrants could get help with the big repairs some wagons needed. Also, we could gather more tools here as well. One of the livery men told me that the fort had gotten more active with all the increase of wagon trains the past year. I sure believed it. Stopping for the next three days, we were all able to stock up on our supplies, rest our stock, and make needed repairs.

Best of all, dear Elizabeth and baby Charles, Fort Hall is where I can finally post my first letter to you! I've

*packed it full with my notes and my love. Please share
these pages with the rest of the family at home. I'll pray it
reaches you as soon as possible and finds you all in good
health. I have no idea how any of you are doing, since
I've had no letters or any other news from home since
leaving there in March. I can't really believe how much
time has already passed.*

*Portneuf River
July 26, 1852
Leaving Fort Hall, we soon passed a large number of clear,
cold pools some fifty or more feet across. From these
sparkling and refreshing pools ran a large stream of water
that united in a few miles with other streams to form the
Portneuf River. To ford the river here, again for our second
time, the captain said we had to raise our wagon beds
nearly to the top of the wagon standards. This was
extremely time consuming, but we all knew it was
necessary to keep our possessions dry and from floating
away.*

*We safely crossed with no major problems or accidents.
Even most of the children were quieter this time. I watched
as one wagon teetered dangerously close to tipping, but
some quick-thinking neighbors were able to jump in the
water fast enough to upright the wagon in time. Also, a
few cows ended up further upstream than was convenient,
but still it was quite a relief to see each near-mishap get
resolved so quickly.*

Shoshone Falls
July 31, 1852
I just got my first sight of the legendary Snake River. We camped on its banks among clouds of hungry mosquitoes. Ever since we reached Bear River weeks ago, the Snake Indians have been numerous, sometimes fairly swarming along our road. They are however quite friendly and pleasant—unlike the mosquitoes!

This is a land of heat and sagebrush. The soil is as dry and light as ashes, and the dust surrounding our every movement is terrible. We camped the second night on a bluff overlooking the Shoshone Falls. As it does for most of its course, the Snake River runs in a very deep canyon here. I know it's the deepest canyon most of us have ever seen. Even though we were close to this great river, the only way to get near it was to go down a rocky, steep cliff for about half a mile. After pondering getting down there for water, we were forced to picture the arduous climb back up the same difficult cliff. This deep canyon was frustrating to those badly in need of water.

That night, instead of settling down like most of the camps were doing, the family closest to our rear, the Clarks, were clearly getting busier after supper. It was twilight when their activity caught my eye. I watched Mr. Clark and their eldest son, Roy, load up with a rope and bucket. Young Roy appeared to be about ten years old.

"Are you going down there now?" I asked, even though I'd already assumed they were. "Aren't you worried about it getting dark?"

Mr. Clark stopped, turned away from his family, and looked at me quite seriously. "We're pretty much desper-

*ate for water, as we just emptied the last of our barrel at
supper. I have to go after more now. Doesn't matter what
time it is. 'Can't ever tell what tomorrow will bring,' my
wife is saying."*

I wrestled with thoughts of volunteering to go with
Clark. In the end my good conscience won, and I sought
out Tim, just to let him know my plans. Finding him
visiting with a few men, I told him, "I'll see you later.
I'm going to help the Clarks fetch some water from the
river below."

Returning to our wagon, I grabbed our empty bucket
and went over to the Clarks. I reported, "I'm going with
you, so let me carry the rope. Here's another bucket we can
use too. Why don't you leave the boy here?"

Will Clark smiled a weary smile and shrugged his
shoulders. "I'd be awfully glad for the help," he said,
handing me his rope. Then turning to Roy, he spoke
firmly. "Now son, your job, is to make sure the family
and animals are safe and resting well when I get back.
Help your mother with anything she asks. I need you to
do that for me, Roy."

"Yes, Pa. I'll do that," the young man said in a
manner that, I couldn't be sure, but it sounded like relief
to me.

Then the two of us men started down the steep
descent. The nearly full moon was rising and gave us the
light we needed. I soon realized we couldn't have made
this trip without that moonlight. It turned out extremely
rough even when we could see our way.

I soon said, "I'm stopping to look here for a stick to
help me with my balance."

After looking around a bit, we each were now equipped with a walking stick. We started off again slowly and carefully stepping down a zigzagged unmarked route, sliding now and then on the loose stones. With a bucket handle around one arm, I felt somewhat limited and off-balance and clumsy. I dearly grabbed on to any outcroppings and trees along the way with the bucket in one hand and the stick in my other.

It was slow going as we each looked for all the handholds we could find. After several slides on my rear end, I wondered how we'd ever get any water to stay in our buckets on the way back up that cliff.

Right about then, as I grabbed at the next patch of tall grass, my heart and hand suddenly froze. I heard an alarming and distinct loud rustling near that very grass in my hand. It seemed only about a foot away. I slowly withdrew my hand inch by inch back to my side. Moving back a step, I motioned for Will to stop and whispered back to him, "Snake, I think."

"Rattler?" he asked.

"Can't say for sure, but sounds big enough to be one. Let me get up above these rocks and see if I can look down at it from there. That's the safest way to check it out, don't you think?" Setting my bucket down carefully and quietly, I started a few steps uphill over to our right side. In about four strides, I could peer down into the rocks and behold, there was the three-foot-long snake. Using my stick, I moved a few smaller rocks to get a look at its tail. That's when it suddenly coiled and posed, ready to strike, like any rattler would!

"Its markings look like a rattler, all right, but I still can't see or hear a rattle," I reported.

It was still curled and ready to strike. Feeling brave from the rocks above it, I reached down and poked the coiled snake with my stick. I pushed at it and then pushed some rocks at it, until it slithered off our pathway and downhill. I never did hear a rattle or see one in that dim light, though.

With relief, I climbed down, saying, "It might not be a rattlesnake. Could've only been a bull snake. Good warning for us, though. We'd better stay on the lookout for any others moving in the evening down to the water."

Now, wiser from my scare, I began first prodding each rocky or bushy place with my stick before putting my hand into unknown territory. Will followed suit, and we kept slowly going diagonally on our path, turning one way and then another. Gradually we made it right down to the river.

The waterfalls were noisy and grand when we got down to them. We both just stared in awe. I had reached the riverbank first. Looking back to check on Will Clark, I could see he was almost on flat ground too. The sound of an eddy's slower-moving water lapping at the rocky shore-line was welcoming. I began taking out my rope and tying it around my bucket handle. It was mainly a precautionary tactic, so as not to lose my bucket.

Turning to Will, I said, "Who wants to go first?"

Will said, "I'm thinking we'd better go one at a time, just in case either of us has trouble. I'll start out."

As he stepped out with his bucket and his stick for balance, he shouted back, "These rocks look slippery, but really they aren't." He was still cautiously moving out from the river's bank, wanting not to stumble. He found a slow, shallow pool larger than most around him and dipped his bucket in and pulled it out. It was mostly full. Standing up straight and adjusting his weight on the rocks, he slowly started back. I watched, and when I could see he was doing well and on firm land again, I moved to the same water hole he'd used and successfully filled my bucket just as he had done. Stepping back beside Will, I blew out a big breath as I set my nearly full bucket down on the land.

"Well, are you ready to tackle the uphill now? And try not to spill our buckets at the same time?" Will asked.

I replied, "Lord help us!"

I knew we'd better keep moving before the present brightness of the moon had a chance to disappear on us. We both turned around, and now Will was in the lead and I followed. Wobbling once or twice, he managed to get his momentum going for the uphill climb.

It was shadowy enough now that we couldn't really see the trail we'd made coming down. The moon still gave us light in some places, and I was very thankful for that. We crept along in a more straightforward ascent than the wide zigzagging we'd done coming down. We didn't have to worry as much going up, but we could still easily slip or slide back down if we weren't careful.

I had to stop to better my grip on the heavy bucket often, manage my balance with my stick, and catch my breath. Struggling with only one hand free to reach ahead, we still tried to use any handholds we could. Neither of us forgot to use the sticks to prod handholds before putting our hands in them.

I'm not quite sure where it was that I ended up in the lead again, but Will took to following my trail when we were about halfway up. Finally, within several yards of the rim, I triumphantly took a huge upward stride of a few feet. I anticipated level ground, but instead of securely stepping up, surprisingly my foot slipped down just as I was pushing hard upward, heaving my body and my precious bucket up to the top. Losing my balance, I fell back and sideways. Unsuccessfully trying to right myself, I hit the ground hard, which then sent my bucketful splashing down my chest. I gasped and groaned, sitting wet and stunned!

Then, righting myself again, I heaved the now mostly empty bucket up on top of the rim. Using my two available hands this time, I pushed myself up next. I sat several moments in despair and shaking my head. Then I realized I'd better get up and help Will. He'd need help getting up here easier than I did.

Near enough now to see me ready and waiting at the rim, Will handed me his bucket. He reached it up, and I grabbed it reaching down. Then he pushed off and pulled himself up alongside me. We both sat there panting. I looked into his bucket to see only half a pail of his water still in there.

I hung my head down between my knees and shook it side to side. I began moaning as we sat. "I just can't believe I spilled it all so near the top! Will, I owe you that water," I said dismally. "You can have some of our water. We have enough to share."

Before he could answer me, the thought I'd just voiced aloud struck me. I started to chuckle, and soon I was loudly laughing. Tim must have heard me, as he and Elik came over to discover Will and me sitting together in the near dark, with me sounding nearly hysterical by now.

Seeing that all three men were staring at me and probably thinking I was delirious, I blurted out amid my laughing, "Now...why...couldn't I...have just thought of that earlier? Before we even went down to the river!"

As Will caught my meaning, he began to shake his head and started to chuckle too. I could see Tim and Elik were staring at the two of us tired-out men like we'd lost our senses.

That's one long, half a night's work I'll never forget. All for a half of a pail of water.

Farewell Bend
August 3, 1852
We passed the wondrous, pounding American Falls. These falls are beautiful, but I still favored the Shoshone Falls for the most astounding views. As we went on to reach the Malheur River, we left the larger Snake River running behind us to our north. Moving along this northeast river route, there weren't any settlements to be seen. It was pleasant enough country, somewhat hot, but it still surprised me that we saw no settlers here. After several more hill crossings, we saw the Snake River again. Here, the river was about twenty feet across with sparkling, clear water that was easy enough to access. This spot was dubbed "Farewell Bend" by previous emigrants, and we

turned from it toward the west. From this point we'd see the mighty Snake River no more as it ran into the beautiful but impassable northern mountains.

We crossed the shallow Burnt River many times over the next three days. I counted eight crossings but may have missed one. The river got its name from the dark, burned hillsides on both shores. The dry grasses outlining this river could catch on fire very easily, so we were told to avoid making any fires.

On the day we left the Burnt River for good, we moved across a huge hill with lovely views on both sides, and going down we entered into the Powder River area. We were crossing beautiful country with distant mountains outlining the horizons. We crossed the western mountains easily and entered into the Grande Ronde Valley and camped there. This valley was a large, open land of rolling grass and streams of water. We rested and restored ourselves here one full day.

Grande Ronde River
August 9, 1852
It was here I found my first Cayuse, a member of a remarkably fine tribe of the so-called "red men." Described by the captain's guidebook as "shrewd and sharp, but always friends of the whites," they were friendly to our group, referring to us as "Boston men." The Cayuse I met was not nearly as curious about me as I was about him. A little further on the trail, I could watch the Cayuse children play as the women worked, grinding corn and preparing fish, and the men sat in small huddles talking.

While staying in this peaceful and beautiful setting called the Grande Ronde area, we rested two more days. We all had plenty of time to observe the chilling Blue Mountains surrounding us. Captain Campbell warned that as tired as we were, we'd soon encounter some of the hardest challenges of the whole trip up in those mountains. Tim, Elik, and I warily looked at each other, and I'm sure that some women started complaining earnestly to their husbands in private soon after that.

Crossing the Blue Mountains
August 11, 1852
Upon entering the Blues, it wasn't long until every person had to dismount their wagon and start walking up the steep incline. Not long after that, most every wagoner was pushing wagons alongside their weary and heavy-laden animals. Next, whole teams were dismantled and doubled up to the next person's team to get just one of the wagons uphill. A few places, more than two teams were needed per wagon to make it up to a safer spot.

Tim and I left Elik in charge of our wagon and helped the nearest neighbors manage their stock and wagons up-hill. Sometimes, we even carried their children. Everyone was taking turns helping the next rear wagon get up as far as their own wagon. In this way, one wagon at a time, we slowly moved along uphill. Also slowed down by the mud below, we covered short distances of only a mile a day.

Finding any clearings large enough for more than one wagon to camp was the next seemingly impossible challenge. Near nightfall, we found a small clearing left by the travelers before us, and after cutting out some more under-growth, three groups called it our camp that night.

I heard tired and cranky children crying as I managed to find a few bites to eat. After those first few bites, I collapsed, falling asleep in my muddy clothes.

Moving down these hills the next day proved just as time-consuming. Now we had to help brake the wagons' wheels, as neither animals nor wagons had control over the slippery downhill pull. In fact, the stock had to be carefully led, as well as the wagons, to prevent them from sliding out of control. Here at this point, putting the weight back in the wagons helped, but most passengers felt too vulnerable riding there and ended up walking again. It was tremendously slow going, one wagon at a time, up and then down these mountains.

Umatilla River
August 13, 1852
After our final summit, we came down a fearfully long hill to the Indian Agency on the Umatilla River. Even moving downhill, this descent took us another day to safely get to the flat lands below. We traveled about three miles along the river and camped. We could see stunning Mount Hood directly west!

Besides the forts we'd encountered, it was here among the Cayuse tribe that we found the first evidence of real civilization we'd seen on the whole trip since leaving the Sauk and Fox Reservations. Since those reservations had been way back in the beginning of our trip, a short distance west of the Missouri River, it was tremendously exciting to me to find some more.

We got fresh potatoes from some Indians. I paid fifty cents for a small washbasin full of small ones, while for a same-size dish of some larger ones, Tim paid a dollar. In another few minutes we heard an old Indian saying, "Little money, little potatoes; big money, big potatoes."

The hills in all directions were covered with wild Indian ponies, or "cayuses," as we later heard them called. Some of their ponies were really fine animals, but the Indians would give four or five of them for one of our American mares. I never figured out why that was.

From here to Fort Dalles, the Oregon Territory was an uninhabited wasteland lying ahead of us. We trudged along for several days with our only consolation that the Cascade Mountains were growing closer.

Chapter 7

*F*ort Dalles
August 18, 1852
*We arrived at Fort Dalles. I was never so grateful to see
the red, white, and blue flying overhead again. Here the
United States government had built a secure and busy fort.*

*Finally, dear family, I am able to post another letter
including more of my notes back home to you! With no
letters waiting for me here, I can only hope to hear from
you still further on, when I get to the Willamette Valley.
I've been told that mail ships get to Fort Vancouver along
the Columbia River and then further in Oregon City,
also. I will patiently wait in hope of a word from home
until I get to Oregon City.*

*At this point, we were told to break down our wagons
into pieces and place them on flat boats so as to float them
down the mighty Columbia River. It is by far the biggest
river we've encountered since leaving the ol' Mississippi
back east.*

*Taking the wagons apart was another time-consuming
job and needed to be done with great care so we'd get the
pieces all to fit and work well when we put them back
together again. We three men began in different parts of*

our wagon. I chose to tackle the wagon tongue. Tim and Elik each worked on a set of wheels.

I carefully studied how the tongue fit back on the wagon as I took it apart, trying to commit to memory the method I'd use to rebuild it. This one piece was of tremendous importance to our immediate future and beyond. The four wheels each took time, but we were all accustomed to dismantling the wheels for repairs and such.

Once dismantled, the broken-down wagons were secured to the wooden rafts and launched from the shore. Each family was riding on their raft, too, and guiding with long poles and a rear rudder. It wasn't easy to watch the first rafts loaded with wary friends and their dear possessions float off down that tremendous Columbia River.

The next day, I was chosen from among those remaining on shore to help drive the cattle down the trail instead of going by raft. Leaving Tim and Elik to float our wagon downriver, I slowly began to help ferry all the wagon train's stock to the north bank above the Columbia's forceful cascades. Thankfully, the cattle wearily trudged on board with little resistance. The horses had to be led by their harnesses, though, since they didn't like the moving raft floor or the many small waves hitting it. It took most of that day getting the cattle and horses all safely over.

Then, we started with the oxen. Getting the first ox on board caused a huge chaos, though. Just as that ox took his very first step onto the raft, another herdsman up ahead hollered at his horse. His yell spooked our ox, who powerfully turned, broke loose, and took off in a run back to the shore. That caused two other oxen to break free and

*follow the first in a swift run. I've never imagined that
oxen could move that fast.*

*Elik, myself, and three other men could hardly keep
the two oxen still near us from bolting, too. With most of
the horses already across the river, it took the other men
time to calm and harness the few horses left. Tim and the
captain took off riding bareback.*

*They managed to get ahead of the spooked oxen,
which were about half a mile away by then. They later
described waving their arms and hats and doing lots of
hollering to get the oxen all turned around. Finally tired
out from so much running, especially after their previous
months of travel, the oxen just ran out of steam and
stopped to graze. They appeared to be calm, like nothing
unusual had ever happened. Others had joined Tim and
Captain Wilson by then and helped guide the wayward
animals back in line again. After that, each ox was hand-
led by two to three men as it was loaded on the ferry. We
got all the remaining stock across by nightfall.*

*Crossing the Columbia River
August 21, 1852
Here, almost in sight of the Promised Land, several
women of our party, who'd withstood the hardships of the
long journey wonderfully well, just gave out and died.
They must have been holding up their weary and frail
bodies in anticipation of making it through the worst to
come. Then, those same tired-out bodies let up that stress
that had kept them moving for so long. Without the stress,
the bodies collapsed. This was the only thing that made*

sense to any of us and was heard from a student of the missionary doctor nearby at Fort Dalles.

Upon getting the word, I returned back to the Columbia's south bank to be among the few emigrants still left there. I joined in the burial procedures for these women. We all grieved at this unexpected loss with a terrible sadness I find hard to describe.

Leaving The Dalles
August 23, 1852
Rejoining the others down past the smoothest and widest part of the Columbia, we spent most of that day again putting our wagons carefully together. Some were very frustrated and blamed others for the puzzling re-mantling job. I, for one, was pleased with how well I remembered the pieces of our tongue. Getting the wagons back together the best we could, we then drove around the cascading falls on the southern side at Fort Dalles. We passed by an Indian cemetery on our way, where we saw bodies in all stages of decay. Some were wrapped up in blankets, some on scaffolds, and some in wigwams. The wigwams were made of broad slabs of cedar covered with carvings and some crude hieroglyphics. All around them the ground was strewn with bones and skulls of the noble red men who had long since passed away. Taken all in all, it was a gruesome sight that I tried not to remember again.

Below Celilo Falls, Oregon
August 26, 1852

Below these falls, our wagons were again taken apart and the families were put aboard several boats to be taken to the mouth of the Sandy River. The Sandy was still over thirty miles west from here. The dismantling was easier after our first experience and only took half a day this time. Our stock were still on the northern side and were led away out into the mountains beyond the mighty Columbia there. Having returned to my job with the stock, I helped drive the animals over the roughest and steepest trails we'd seen yet, and it was much more work than I'd expected. We struggled along, urging the tired animals to climb over fallen logs, go around large stones, and walk up and down slopes. I found myself feeling sorry for the creatures, who couldn't understand any of this at all.

After several days, my group, along with our stock, trekked down to the river's shoreline. We were all extremely happy to see our friends camped near the mouth of the Sandy River. We and the cattle were once more ferried across to the south side, where men, women and children, and all the wagons had already safely landed. It was among the cheers and backslapping regarding our safety and reunion that some first heard of the recent deaths of the women we'd buried near Fort Dalles. Sadness crept into the rejoicing now and overtook our group. Many were awash in grief, so we camped another day in this pleasant riverside setting.

Sandy River
September 2, 1852

Once more all together again, there was nothing in the way of us reaching the Willamette Valley. Sadly, it was here that Elik said his goodbyes, along with ten families and three other single men. These folks were all heading further west to Fort Vancouver. The fort would be their next stop before turning and going up northward.

Standing beside his mare and pack horse, Elik said, "I wish you both the very best. You've been good travel mates, and it's hard to move on without you. However, too many others are going to get in your way down there, finding that gold ahead of you." He smiled. "I've got to get away from those crowds while I still can."

We shook hands, and Tim and I each grasped his arm somberly. I finally replied, "May God go with you and keep you safe. I want to see you again if you ever come south."

And with that, Tim and I let go of Elik's arm. He mounted his horse, turned it around, and off Elik rode with his two animals. We were deeply sobered by this separation, despite having known it was coming for the past month.

Oregon City
September 3, 1852
Tim and I headed south with many others. The very next day, we traveled the muddy, wide trail into Oregon City, the town we'd heard so much about when back east. Most folks I knew considered this the end of the trail. The town seemed enormous and overwhelming to me, with many businesses ready and waiting to supply our needs. There

were churches, stores, parks, doctors, and everything we could want. I saw a lumber mill on the edge of the Willamette, and about three streets further on, there was a flour mill in operation.

Riding alongside Tim, my eyes watered as I thought about God's goodness to me as here we were safely in the Oregon Territory at last. We'd arrived just five months after leaving home in Missouri.

Chapter 8

Oregon City

*We supped at a restaurant in one of the biggest hotels on
Main Street. Having someone else cook for us bachelors
that night was a treat worth any amount of money. The
owner stopped at our table to visit a bit. With pride he
said, "Welcome to the first incorporated town in Oregon
and the Territory's largest city." He claimed this was now
a city of about 1,000 people, of which I didn't doubt.*

*He also gave us friendly directions to the south of town
where we should set up our camp. Riding along with our
wagon, we saw that the whole town was only about three
to four streets deep, due to towering cliffs that rose over the
narrow lowlands. The long, thin town stretched from north
to south along the east shore of the river.*

*We slept well and long. The next morning my hopes
were riding high to get some word from home, so locating
the post office was the first thing on my mind. I got
directions from the livery owner near our camp. He'd been
leaning against his doorframe watching all of us newcomers
coming and going. Following his directions was easy, and
there it was, just one block off Main Street—an established post office!*

Even early in the morning, there were others already waiting in line; to me they looked as eager as I felt. Finally when my turn arrived, I spoke up: "Looking for mail for James Bushnell," and waited. I couldn't stop shifting from foot to foot. The man returned and said kindly, "I'm sorry, we aren't able to find any letters for you."

That meant there were no letters from you, dear Elizabeth, nor from Mother.

Now, I tried, "Do you have any word about a William Bushnell, my brother? He's been here over a year, and we still haven't heard anything from him."

That was another big disappointment. Reluctantly turning and going back outside, still dazed, I had to swallow down my discouragement. It seemed the Bushnell name was unknown around here. Forcing myself out of further despairing thoughts, I slowly continued walking down the dirt street and began talking to any folks along my route.

"Hello, my name is James Bushnell. I've just arrived in town, as you can pretty much tell. Have you lived here long?" Then I said, "I'm looking for any news about my brother William Bushnell? I hope some the locals may have run into him."

Without any encouragement from those to whom I spoke, I soon gave up. I'd covered the length of that street and the next major street without any results. I told myself that at least the Bushnell name had now been heard of around here!

So without a bit of news from home, I returned to camp and started helping Tim, who was cleaning and checking through all our equipment. While sweeping off our dusty canvas top and standing on the outside of the wagon bed to do it, I decided that I'd return to the post office on the morrow. Then I'd mail the remainder of this journal to you. With that chore done and that decision made, I spent the rest of that day looking through the closest general stores and purchased some fresh food and nonperishables.

After packing these supplies in our wagon, I decided I still had time to go watch the men working at the docks. When I told Tim my plans, he decided he was ready for an afternoon nap instead and let me go it alone.

There were several steamships that ran from Portland to Oregon City and then back to the north, and fewer others to Salem to our south. I enjoyed watching men in rowboats carting supplies out to one ship named the Lot Whitcomb. I assumed that it was owned by a local ship builder. I remembered observing a busy shipyard north of the falls when coming into town.

About a dozen men were on the wharf loading local apples, potatoes, a variety of wheats, and some fresh green beans into boxes for shipping. I knew I'd bought plenty of apples, but the smell of those green beans made my mouth water. Interrupting the closest man loading the beans, I asked, "Where can I buy myself some of those beans?"

In a friendly manner he stood up, looked me over while smiling, and replied, "Two streets over that way, at the store called Abernathy's. That's my employer. Be sure to tell him that I sent you in. Any nice word may earn me some good favor." He smiled cheerfully as he wiped his brow.

"I sure will, and thanks for the help." Taking off in

*the direction he'd pointed out, I easily found that big
general store. Entering Abernathy's double doors, I quickly
realized how immense it was. It was bigger than stores we
had back home and even larger than some of the ones I'd
seen in Hannibal.*

*Slowly browsing the first aisle, which was lined with
pots, pans, and other cooking supplies, I admired the
newness of them. Quickly enough I decided it wasn't
frugal to just keep looking at so many fancy items. I deli-
berately turned to the fresh produce area. I bagged up some
fresh beans out of a barrel using the paper supplied for
shoppers. I added some fresh beets too. These would both
keep well for our journey, although I was pretty sure the
beans would be eaten soon enough. I added some more salt
to my purchases and got out of there, trying not to look at
or smell anything else tempting.*

*We ate well that night and especially enjoyed the
salted beans. After another good night's sleep in the mild
weather, I got up the next day with a purpose. I was
mailing my journal home today, and that was foremost on
my mind.*

*Walking back to the postmaster's office, I silently
prayed, God, help this safely reach my loved ones back
home. I handed my precious, fairly large bundle of papers
to the older woman behind the desk that time. I watch her
carefully tie my papers together and then weigh them upon
a fine scale. I gulped when she turned back to me and
asked for $2.00. Now this bundle was suddenly more
precious as I reluctantly counted out some of my meager
remaining funds. I watched her put our address on it and*

*then carefully set it in a leather bag that said "Missouri"
on the outside tag.*

*Within those few minutes, my journal was out of my
hands and on its way to Elizabeth. I prayed again for it to
find them all safe and happily waiting for my news thus
far on the trip. I was then thinking the worst of the travels
were behind me. It's a very good thing that I didn't know
the perils that still lay ahead.*

Chapter 9

Elizabeth

April 1853

Elizabeth would never, ever have dreamt that she would be doing this. That she'd sold their farm and joined a wagon train heading out west with a baby and no husband was still hard to believe. However, she'd actually done it!

She hadn't heard from James since he'd left for the California gold mines in March of last year; it was many months longer than she'd expected to wait. Over time she'd convinced herself that James must be too poor—or worse even ill, hurt, or in some kind of danger—if he hadn't made it home by now. With no news to go on, she'd fretted over and over about all the possibilities of what could've happened to him. His mother had been worrying too.

The long, tiring summer and brief fall had kept her busy running their farm. Their corn and hay fields had only done marginally well. The potatoes were small, and the alfalfa field never grew more than a few inches high. Her vegetable garden had become bug infested too, and as hard as she'd tried to control the spiders, weevils, and aphids, she hadn't won that fight. She'd needed plenty of help from Jason, Cory, and Mother Bushnell, plus a few neighbors, to get her meager crops harvested.

Then, following the first tough spring, summer, and fall, the early winter days and following months had been even worse. Being stuck in her home due to storm after storm, she'd been unable to keep up with everything outdoors. She relied on Jason or Cory to get her stock and animals tended most days. Visiting with any friends had been put off way too often because the harsh wind and snowstorms were so hard to travel in with a baby.

That long, tedious winter had caused her such discontent, she'd started listening to Jason's talk of going out west too. Starting in January, he'd proposed almost daily, "Let's all go together and look for James and William." As he talked about it more and more, she heard him saying, "We can start our own homesteads together with the free land promised to adults who settle out in the Oregon Country. Between the four of us, I bet we'd get 720 acres all together." This new beginning sounded so promising after their recent hard Missouri winters. Jason, being a lot like his older brother James, had kept repeating this new, adventurous plan to her whenever he came to help out.

One thing she knew: by the end of that February, she'd had enough of farm life here in Missouri—especially like this, all on her own. Their farm had barely produced enough to support just the two of them from the spring to the fall. They'd only scraped by this past winter because of Jason's help. With the way the frozen ground still looked now in March, it was going to be a very small growing season, probably producing a slight summer crop again. If Jason and Mother were going to sell and move out west, Elizabeth certainly didn't plan to stay behind and work these eighty acres all alone!

When most of the Bushnells finally decided to leave, she'd sold the farm to their new neighbors, the Adams, without much further thought. With a part of the proceeds, she'd bought three yokes of oxen and one yoke of cows. Jason and Cory had furnished the wagon. The two brothers, Elizabeth, baby Charles, and Mother Bushnell had all packed up their most necessary and precious belongings, the supplies necessary for their trip of several months, and what they thought they needed on their future farms. All this had to fit in the Conestoga wagon and their four saddlebags.

It was especially sad to watch Mother ponder what furniture and household goods she had to leave behind. After raising her family and having a large house for the last ten years, she had many more nice things to part with than Elizabeth. The piano had to stay here, of course, and the oak hutch that held the family china would have to stay. In regards to the bed frames, tables, and some nice china, it was much harder for Mother to decide. Elizabeth didn't know what to say as she saw her mother-in-law's eyes fill with tears more than once while planning. Elizabeth and James had some nice items that had mostly been wedding presents and some precious baby items that Elizabeth would take. As most of their furniture was simple and hand-made, it would be left. She would miss it, but James could always make some more for them out west. Together the two women carefully packed up their dishes in as much protection as possible using bed sheets and clothing. They set aside cooking utensils and some old dishes for their traveling use.

When the day came to pack their wagon, the one big bed frame went in first, and everything else was packed in barrels, baskets, or loosely around that bed. Linens and some clothing were packed between two mattresses, and then all of the bedding went on top, plus all of the pillows, quilts, and heavy coats. The bed made a very soft, high resting place for the women. Baby Charles had an area blocked off for his bed between the steamer chest and the wagon corner. Elizabeth had feared he'd fall off the big high bed, as he was only used to his contained cradle. She also knew he'd do better corralled somewhere when it was time for him to sleep.

They hung as many things as they could on hooks inside the wagon frames, and lots of their things fit under the animal feed and buckets. The water barrel was secured on the outside by ropes to the right side of the wagon bed, and the butter churn was tied on the left side. Jason had been told that the rough wagon ride was supposed to actually churn their butter by the end of a day or two.

If it really worked, Mother said she'd be glad to have one less chore to do on the trip. Elizabeth and Mother placed their cooking utensils and items near the back, as when the tailgate came down, they would have their cooking surface and make-do table space. Most of the larger pots and pans and other cooking items could be hung on the rear wooden frames that supported the canvas top, too, for cooking convenience.

Brother George came to help them pack up. Only this oldest Bushnell brother had held out against his family's pressures and still wasn't convinced to try for "the better life." He was staying in Adair County on his own farm. He persisted in taking no such chances as the others were doing. He liked his situation.

Sister Helen was staying put here, too, with her husband, Frank. Frank was building a gristmill, and they were hoping it would become their big advantage over farming. They arrived with their two boys about midday to oversee the final packing and be there for the inevitable departure.

After the wagon was packed and stock prepared, there wasn't anything left to do but get a start that same day on the way to Independence, their taking-off point. The tears flowed from the three women and most of the men as they said their sad goodbyes. Only little Charles remained cheerful as he gave out his wet baby kisses. Elizabeth couldn't help wondering if she'd ever see George, Frank, or Helen again. Nobody spoke that thought aloud.

Instead Elizabeth said, "I know you'll get out to see us as soon as possible. Cory predicts there'll be railroads running to the west just about as soon as we make it there. Either a train or a stagecoach would make it a nice trip for you to come visit. Or we can come back and see you once we get settled with our farms up and going."

"Yes," they all quickly affirmed and hugged again. After Mother was helped up to the wagon seat, Jason handed baby Charles up to her. Charles giggled and waved to his cousins. Now it was Elizabeth's turn to take the big step in order to climb up. What a big step she and little Charles were making.

Chapter 10

James

Leaving from Oregon City, James, Tim, and several other families they knew headed south for Salem. The good, flat farmland farther down the valley was calling out to some. For the others it was the allure of gold in the southerly hills that motivated them. With the smoothly worn road leading them, it took just another day to reach Salem. They arrived there on the ninth day of September, 1852.

Walking around several streets, James observed stores with food and home goods, some food packing plants, livery stables, hotels, and even a newspaper. Salem gave both Tim and James the feel of a larger city again, as had Oregon City. After resting in the cheapest hotel for the next two days, they'd gathered as much information about the gold mining areas as they could. They talked to many miners that were coming into town and some going out to return to their mining. They also bought the last of their necessary supplies here in Salem.

The evening of the second day, James said to Tim, "I've had enough of city life already. I'm anxious to get on to the gold! First thing tomorrow, I'm ready to sell my wagon and any tools we don't need. Are you with me?"

Tim was ready too, and they started planning how they'd lighten their load for the rough travel into the foothills. The next day, they both began selling off many of their remaining possessions. The smaller items went quickly, but they still had the wagon and team left. At breakfast the next morning, James asked around the hotel dining table for any ideas. An older man told James, "Speak to a Mr. Flem Hill. He's come into town from his ranch near Winchester. That's up the Umpqua River. He might be needing some more equipment like yours."

James quickly thanked him and grabbed Tim. They hurried off to find this Mr. Hill, who was staying at a friend's house in town. They found him there all right, and an hour later they'd sold the wagon, the oxen, and some unnecessary tools to Mr. Hill. However, there was just one obstacle to complete the deal.

"Well, my problem is I've got two wagons to get back home," complained Mr. Hill. To help sell their deal, James and Tim offered to drive their team and wagon along with Mr. Hill back to his home. They should have asked where he lived before being so agreeable.

James and Tim began their five-day journey to Mr. Hill's place, which was west and south of Salem. James said to Tim as they rode together, "At least we're heading in the right direction. Since I wasn't smart enough to ask how far away he lived, I could've gotten us way off our course going the wrong way."

Tim pleasantly replied, "I guess we might as well enjoy the diversion and see what this country has to offer us besides gold."

"I can't argue with that, although I was more than ready to go after all the gold waiting for us out in those hills," James said. Inwardly, he was thinking that Tim's cooperative attitude made him appreciate his friend once again. Tim was growing more endearing to James with each step of their adventurous enterprise. He smiled and said, "Thanks, Tim, for sticking with me."

Passing through meadows and seeing many young fruit trees made very pleasant scenery for the newcomers. Mr. Hill said, "This is the Long Tom River," as they passed along its west side. The river flowed lazily along beside them, and the air was full with the autumn smells and the sun's warmth. Leaving the river, they followed Mr. Hill southeast on an easy ride for three more days. Camping in the lush, grassy meadows along low hillsides those next two nights gave James a deep appreciation for this lovely, fertile-looking country.

He said dreamily to Tim, "I can easily imagine settling down to homestead here in these beautiful lowlands. If I had a mind to farm again."

"Do you?" Tim asked somberly.

With a reassuring smile, James said, "No, not now. I'd still rather pursue the gold fields with you. I can't think about settling down yet. After we get our gold, then I'll make that decision—about where Elizabeth and I will settle down."

The third day after leaving the Long Tom River behind them, they finally reached the town of Winchester. After reaching Mr. Hill's home a few miles out, they decided to stay there several more days, as it seemed a good spot to discuss their trip south with some of the locals. They'd been given lots of advice as soon as they were introduced around. Mr. Hill and his neighbors provided them with maps and shared stories and hopefully some real facts from miners they knew. These men also talked with a lot of other settlers traveling through there, and that helped too.

Tim and James pored over the maps collected for them. James wrote down what they learned from listening to men who'd been living here several years already. Then, when Tim and James had planned enough and organized their supplies again, they were ready to depart for their first mining adventure.

Just as the two young men were ready to leave, though, a wise neighbor said, "I'd advise you to sell your worn, tired-out mares here. Go get a cayuse pony from the Indian camp over that next hill there. Their ponies are sturdier. They're specially bred for speed and endurance in this land around here. Those cayuse are already accustomed to all these hills."

James and Tim listened to him and immediately turned toward the Indian camp. They'd been assured that the Indians were friendly and eager to trade. As they rode into the camp, James noticed quite a few teepees. These were made from reeds woven into mats and then formed into walls. The Indian women looked up as the strangers passed but kept working the cooking fires near their teepees. Several children ran up to Tim and James, and most of the men within sight of them stood up.

Pulling their horses up to the closest group of men, James and Tim dismounted. In slow English, Tim said, "We want to trade for two ponies." As he spoke, he held up two fingers and pointed to a group of ponies standing in a crudely made corral. James decided to just smile and nod, looking as pleasant as he could for this exchange.

Tim was met with grunts of affirmation, nods, and movement. The whole group strode over to the ponies. A younger man said, "Your horses, two ponies?" And with those few words, they each bought a cayuse pony, giving up their mares in the deal.

Getting back to Mr. Hill's on their much smaller rides made for some good laughs between James and Tim. They eventually adjusted to their feet being so close to the ground by the time they reached the Hills'. By then, James decided to just call his pony Cayuse.

They packed up their tools, boards for their mining rocker, blankets, tent, and other provisions into two sets of leather saddlebags. Then they stopped and said their grateful goodbyes to these helpful new Winchester friends. James had especially enjoyed this friendly community.

James and Tim rode off side by side heading for the gold fields of southern Oregon. Realizing his dream was finally being fulfilled, James suddenly rode up close to Tim and, grasping his shoulder, said, "I'm not going to forget the thrill in this moment, Tim. We're really off to the gold fields!"

Tim grinned in reply and shouted out, "Heehaw!" He kicked his pony into a trot and waved his hat in the air.

Chapter 11

Within the same day, James and Tim came upon the Rogue River, the biggest river they'd seen since they'd left the Willamette. After a brief discussion, they decided to camp a few days on this scenic, sparkling river and try out their mining skills. They weren't alone more than just the one day, though. On the second morning, as they worked their pans along the rocky shore, three old Indians rode into their camp, grunted a greeting, and dismounted. Surprised and alarmed, James and Tim each stood and faced the strangers.

One of the eldest-looking men grunted another greeting that sounded pleasant enough. Stammering, Tim responded, "Hello." That same man motioned for Tim and James to both keep on panning. James and Tim looked at each other, and James said, "I'll watch your back while you do as they say. I guess just show them how we're doing the panning?"

Nodding in agreement, Tim went back to his riverbank spot and continued to pan along the shore. All three of the Indians got closer to Tim and watched him as though mesmerized. There were a few non-English words passed among the red men as they stood there, certainly nothing Tim nor James could understand. After about thirty minutes or so, one of the visitors offered James some type of root he pulled out from his leather bag. James took it and cautiously ate a couple of bites. He offered some to Tim.

James commented, "It tastes something like an onion," then smiled and nodded his approval to the Indian men. They grinned back at him and offered them both some more.

The Indians sat down on the grass and motioned for the young men to join them. They all shared a lunch of the onion-tasting root, some beef jerky, and bread. James ladled up some water for each of them. After washing down their lunches, the two white men weren't sure what they should do. As if understanding this uncertainty, the red men muttered their strange words amongst themselves again. Then the elder stared at James and began gesturing.

"Tim, what do you think he's saying?"

"It seems he may want us to go with them or to follow them. They sure seem friendly, and they for sure know more about this river than we do. I'm interested in their help, and we could learn from their company. Do you think they're safe, James?"

James thoughtfully and slowly responded, "Well, I think we should go with them a ways and see what it is they're wanting to show us."

Tim and James decided to take their chances. After packing up some of their gear and stashing it inside their tent for safety, they mounted their ponies and followed the Indians' directions.

After heading uphill and leaving the river, they were on a rocky bank that ran alongside the canyon. Following this embankment and their new friends, they came to a small Indian camp of what seemed about twenty adults. They were met and greeted by most of the men in the camp with friendliness and curiosity. To Tim and James's surprise, they didn't stop. They

were motioned on through this camp by their Indian guides. A
few of the more curious men from this village began to follow,
too.

They traveled about an hour going slightly uphill. They
passed through another Indian camp of similar size as the first
one. James and Tim often looked at each other, and Tim
muttered, "I think we've become a parade."

At the end of their second hour, they came to a large,
flattened knoll that overlooked a spectacular view of the Rogue
River valley. From here they were astonished to see spread out
before them three more Indian camps. Each of these three all
appeared much larger than their previous encounters. The red
men here were spread more thickly than either Missourian had
ever imagined.

Their original guides took them into the middle camp. James
and Tim were stopped in front of a youth who'd apparently
acquired some broken English. He told them that these were
the Takelma Indians. After a brief discussion through hand
motions and a few basic words, they were invited to camp here
among the Takelmas. Talking it over, James and Tim agreed to
accept the Indians' hospitality. James especially wanted to remain
on friendly terms with so many strangers surrounding them.

Then it became quite a show as the two white men tried to
mimic riding back and gathering up the rest of their equipment.
They finally got their hosts to understand that they needed to
go back before they could actually set up camp with them.

Two of the red men quickly volunteered to escort Tim and
James back. Again, Tim looked questioningly at James and muttered, "They'd better have good intentions, or we're in deep
trouble now."

Solemnly, James could only nod in agreement and send a

silent prayer upward for God's safekeeping and the wisdom to know if they were in trouble. Taking off back the same way they had come, the four men reached their mining camp within another two hours. Sensing no danger so far, the white men dismounted and offered their two guests some pork sausage they'd bought in Salem. The Indians tasted it cautiously. After about two bites, they gestured wildly for something to drink. After gulping down water ladled from the barrel, they didn't seem interested in any more sausage.

The Indians watched in fascination as Tim and James began dismantling the mining rocker and tying the wooden pieces, along with their pickaxes, together onto the ponies' saddlebags. When it came to taking down the tent, the men even helped James and Tim fold it up. The Indians carefully fingered and examined the canvas as they held it, as though it was a rare treasure. After packing up all of their gear, they all headed back to the Takelmas' camp again. Tim and James were relieved that this had gone without any incident.

This camp they went back to was home to about fifty cooking fires and lean-to homes. Walking through the encampment, James noticed that some of the younger men scowled and glowered at them. This was the first sign of anything but friendly curiosity among these Indians, and it surprised James. These same young men refused any attempts at conversation and refused to even sit down with the two visitors. James wondered again why he sensed such hostility coming from those half dozen men.

Most members of the tribe, though, were very interested in James and Tim and tried some limited conversation. Using their hands and sketching in the dirt, Tim and James asked more about the Rogue River's flow and where exactly they were on the river. After they understood the Indians' directions, they thanked them the best they could. Then the Indians started describing other white men who'd passed through this way. These new Indian friends seemed extremely curious about all the white men who came to their land in search of gold. There were some head shakes and disgusted-sounding grunts whenever James or Tim asked a gold-related question. James soon realized the Indians didn't value the gold around them at all.

Apparently bored with the talk of gold, the red men soon stood up and led the guests to some small fields around the camps. Gesturing, they proudly showed off their small crop of potatoes and another crop they called "camas." At this place, James and Tim realized it was this vegetable they'd eaten in the morning. In these two small fields, eight women and six older children were at work. The men, who were so eager to show off their planted fields, didn't stay there long, though. They turned everyone back to camp and motioned for them to sit down again.

That was when the two white Americans started noticing that the women here did the majority of the work. It seemed that the men sat in groups talking most of the day. James did observe three men fishing along the creek bank for a bit. However, he saw the fishermen bring their catches back for their women to clean and to cook for them.

Later on, some of those women brought this freshly cooked fish for their group of men to enjoy. It was a welcome change of menu for the two white men, who hadn't eaten any fish since leaving the Snake River. Watching and copying how their guests tore into the fish, James enjoyed his fish and three small potatoes. He was thirsty, but as the red men weren't drinking anything, he decided not to ask. He could get water from his own gear later.

After spending two very interesting days observing the Indians' way of life, James and Tim packed up, said their good-byes, and withdrew from the Indian camp as gracefully as they could. With a few new friends following them, they rode into the next set of rolling hills. One of the next big hills was dubbed Gold Hill, as the Indians had managed to explain to them. Near Gold Hill, they found a bend where the Rogue slowed down to a crawl and seemed to have some promising prospects. They discovered after a short stroll that they were below some smaller rapids and were so pleased with this spot that they settled in there. The Indians silently watched them set up camp again.

The tent went up easily, and their rocker was smoothly put back together. They shared a quick meal with their friends around the campfire. James was relieved when the Indians finally stood as the sun set and were ready to go back to their own camp. Saying another round of goodbyes, Tim and James were freely on their own once again.

They began work the next morning. They started by taking turns bringing in heavy pans full of sandy water and rinsing them through the rocker's slopes. One would haul water for a spell, and the other would work the rocker, moving it like its namesake to keep the water moving and draining out. Then they'd trade positions, always carefully stretching their backs and other sore muscles first. As they each practiced their gold panning techniques, James enjoyed the sun's warmth and the sweet music of the rippling rapids at this place. Awkward at first, they soon eased into the rhythm of pouring water that was then followed by the rocker's creaks and swooshes.

As pleasant as this routine became to them, after a week they'd found only a few sparkling gold flecks. Tim was the first to say, "That's it! I'm not interested in staying here any longer. We've got to find something more promising. Let's go farther on."

James didn't argue any with Tim. They packed their belongings and headed southeast. Without stopping overnight, the two men arrived at the community of Jacksonville. This was the newly formed Jackson County seat. They'd learned back in Winchester that it was also the main headquarters of Oregon gold mining. Gold had been discovered in Jackson Creek just the previous winter. Rumors were that the first few claims each pulled out several ounces of gold a day. Many miners had moved in and were still getting some promising results.

James and Tim looked over this busy town that appeared to have about a thousand residents. After riding several blocks into town, James observed aloud, "It seems to be only men around this place." Obviously many other fellows had left their families behind to pursue adventure just as they had.

After many more observations over the next few days, James wondered, *Are any of these actually family men at all?* Their language, manners, and coarse stories indicated a lack of the family values with which James was familiar. These miners were unlike most men he'd ever known, and they made him uncomfortable.

Another disturbing event occurred around the dining table that first night in their hotel. One fellow loudly told everyone, "The troop of soldiers you saw roaming around town all today are reporting some terrible Indian attacks. Two of the big mining camps up Jackson Creek have been havocked. All their tents, sheds, and equipment were destroyed by vicious red men.

The escapees said they'll never forget the shrieking and cries of those Indians. No one was harmed, but the warning and intent was still fierce and menacing. They can't be trusted anymore!"

James and Tim looked at each other in shock. Another alarmed hotel guest immediately urged, "We need to get some men and weapons organized to retaliate and take care of those savages!"

As some of the others started to agree with him, it was Tim who spoke up most loudly and calmly. In a cautioning tone, he said, "Our experience—James's and mine—tells a different story, men. We met a friendly and welcoming tribe just a few days ago. They invited us to stay at their encampment, which we did for two days. We found them very helpful. We both always felt safe there. I know those Indians can be trusted."

He continued, "I'm sure this attack was led by just a few unhappy Indians who don't like being disturbed. There are so many friendly and cooperative red men, how could you really strike back at the right Indians without harming the innocent ones? We have to be careful, men, and heed those warnings they gave us, sure enough. However, retaliating against all the Indians, whether they're guilty or innocent, is just going to cause more uprisings and much more harm for all of us."

James quickly affirmed Tim's sound advice, but was startled to see that most didn't agree. It was disheartening to James and Tim to realize they were in the minority among their fellow hotel guests. They saw how deeply the distrust, disrespect, and hate ran toward all Indians. It was much more hate than James had ever encountered on the Oregon Trail or back home. Most of these Jacksonville folks were way beyond being reasonable.

Despite the grumbling and alarm about Indian attacks, James and Tim stayed in the Jacksonville area and prospected in the streams nearby for almost two weeks. The weather was clear, sunny, and not too warm. James often remarked to Tim how beautiful and pleasant this part of southern Oregon seemed, and Tim agreed. The countryside was a dried-up golden brown in many spots, but there was always a wooded knoll or shady creek bed nearby. The falling autumn leaves sparkled in the sun and colored the hillsides. All this, in addition to cheerful streams splashing over sparkling rocks and making nature's music, was magnificent to James.

Despite all this natural beauty, they found so little gold that they were finally motivated to travel farther southeast, over to Applegate Creek. Some of the Applegate miners they'd met back in town had been mining here quite a while, and earlier they'd invited them into their camp.

The men they met up with on the Applegate told them more stories about mining adventures, wild animals, Indians, and the many settlers coming through. When discussing the hundreds of settlers passing near here, one old man declared, "I heard firsthand that there are new roads and trails being used by more and more of the wagon trains. Some wagon trains are heading for the middle or southern valley, and some are departing the main trail and heading for the California region. The fields and towns in the mid-valley will be filled up soon enough."

James only listened half-heartedly, as he didn't really care much about anything else but his finding some gold around here. Much later, it would occur to him that this man was correct.

After a week on the Applegate, they still had no success. It was wearing on James's spirit. So he wasn't too surprised when one afternoon Tim abruptly stood up, threw off his hat, and shouted out, "Greenhorns! I have no idea what we're doing wrong, but there must be something to this we haven't learned yet. I don't think I can handle much more of it, James. I feel every bit the greenhorn they call us, even though it's been over a month now."

James didn't know how to respond, since Tim was right. After finishing washing through the load in front of him, he stood up slowly and said, "Yeah, it is frustrating, all right. And you're sure right about us not having any success yet. Despite our efforts and hard work, it's real discouraging."

After another moment, James asked Tim, "Are you ready to try our luck farther on, going into California? Maybe we should've just stuck with our original plan to head there first. Anyways, I say let's keep going south and hope for better luck. What do you think?"

"I'm ready," Tim replied gruffly. They both picked up their pans and rockers then and there and headed back to their campsite.

"I'll cook up some dinner and some other food for traveling," said James. Agreeing to that, Tim cleaned off their tools then laid them out to organize for packing. After eating, cleaning up thoroughly, and doing some packing, they went to bed with hopes of better luck soon to come.

The weak sun had risen above the foothills by the time they finished up their last packing and rode off on heavily loaded ponies once again. Passing through hills and valleys on their way south, they hurried on into northern California.

In the next few days, they crossed snow-dusted trails in the Siskiyou Mountains. They followed a well-used Indian trail over these mountains that led them down south to Scott River and then farther south to the Trinity River. Scott River was claimed to be an ore-producing river by some locals there, and James and Tim were tempted to stop. After discussing it, Tim convinced James that they needed more than these rumors to set up camp again.

They arrived dirty and saddle-worn into Shasta City, California, in the first days of October. It was just out of Shasta City that James would soon get one of the biggest surprises of his trip.

Chapter 12

After cleaning up and resting for two days in the rapidly growing city of Shasta, they found it an ample source for restocking a few supplies. Most of the townspeople were helpful and friendly with advice for "the greenhorns." The attitude here in town was if the miners were successful, they'd be back spending their money in their town first.

James and Tim left Shasta City astride their faithful, sturdy ponies with high hopes, renewed supplies, and fresh outlooks. Following the dirt road, they passed near a community called Middleton but didn't stop. Soon they overtook a small group of miners on the same dirt road they'd chosen going out of Middleton. These miners looked freshly stocked, as they were loaded up with many bundles. James assumed they must have just purchased all their winter supplies back in town.

Cheerfully, Tim called out a hello, as he was ahead of James. The miners turned their heads and acknowledged the two followers, but their greeting was hardly cordial. Without signs of warmth or friendliness, these miners slowly stopped, turned back slightly, and instead of a greeting began to question the newcomers.

"Where are you two headed?" the rear horseman asked

warily. Before Tim could answer, another one harshly interrupted, "Have you ever been in these parts before?"

James had pulled up behind Tim, and now he replied, smiling as he spoke. "We're only two greenhorns trying out our luck and could sure use some wise directions. I bet you fellas can set us on a path so as we won't get in your way. Why, in all this open space, there looks to be plenty of room for us all."

As James was talking, one of these rough-looking strangers, the one with the most hair on his face, caught his attention. James directed his next question to him. "Which way do you suggest we head, you there, riding on the pinto?"

That bearded man on the pinto turned his head to see James more directly and replied in a voice so familiar that it shook James from head to foot. "Well, we're headed over to the Cottonwood Creek area."

That man's voice and his bearing convinced James he'd come very unexpectedly upon his own brother, William! Surprise momentarily overcame him. Then he hastily dismounted, rushed over, and tried to pull that man down from his horse. Grabbing the man's strong arm and shoulder, he shouted, "William Bushnell! It's me, your little brother James!"

As if frozen, William resisted and just stared down at James speechlessly. Then he relaxed and gave in to James's pull. Quickly jumping down, he hollered over to his companions, "Boys, get down here and meet my baby brother!"

The freeze in the air suddenly broke as warmth gushed out amid many more cheerful exclamations. Two brothers from Missouri suddenly meeting up like this out here in California was stunning to all of them. Lots of introductions were made, and then William started explaining himself.

He told James, "When I got out here over a year ago, I

chose to go directly south to California. The mining reports were more positive, and I found good company to ride along with. We've had some good and bad luck here, but we aren't ready to quit. We just got resupplied back in Shasta for another winter's worth of work."

He paused and then asked, "How come you're out here? Did any other brothers come with you? Did Mother get the letters I sent, James? I sent two back home after arriving in Jacksonville last year."

"No. Sorry to tell you that we never heard a word. It was hard on all of us wondering why that was. It took plenty of faith to keep believing that after a year's silence you were still alive and well. Ma was especially worried that you were in trouble. I kept assuring her that it was probably just some simple reason that kept us from hearing anything. We boys kept Ma's spirits up the best we could."

"Oh, I'm so sorry to hear it. It grieves me deeply that I upset Mother," William sighed.

Hearing his brother's grief, James turned the conversation to his own explanation. "I left everyone else back home still farming. I left to try mining with Tim. I hope you remember Tim from my Hannibal trip?"

Both brothers turned. Tim smiled back and said hello again to William.

"Jason and Cory and Mother are helping Elizabeth keep the farm going until I get back there with my gold," James continued. "We fellows left home in March on a mighty big wagon train. We parted with our friend Elik, who was heading north from the Columbia. The two of us just pulled into Oregon City and then took off to start our mining in the southern Oregon area. We haven't been lucky anywhere we've been yet. Tim says we're still too green." James chuckled.

"It looks like you and your friends know what you're doing, William," Tim said. "What are your next plans?"

Not to be deterred yet, William turned back to James. "Catch me up with all the family news! Is everyone well? How are the farms doing?"

Just as James was about to reply, he noticed the other men standing around starting to shift restlessly, and he hesitated. And then, James suddenly had a new idea form within him. He said, "William, let's take a moment over by that oak tree in private." William shrugged his shoulders questioningly, but strode over to the tree with James. James continued, "Would you consider taking Tim and me on as your new partners? We could use your mining advice. I know it's a lot to ask all of a sudden like this. We're only a month into mining ourselves, but we're strong, hard workers and quite determined," he added quickly.

William was silent. James watched him put his hand under his shaggy chin and stroke his beard. Then, slowly nodding his head and smiling, he said, "I can do that. I'll commit to this fall and winter with you two fellows."

After this quick consultation between the brothers, William turned and walked back to his friends. "Fellas, I've changed my plans and am going along with these two greenhorns. I'll be parting with you from here on. They certainly could use my help, and I feel obliged to take them on. Any one of you are welcome to come along with us, though. I hope you understand that my family has to come first in this."

James then realized he hadn't even asked Tim about his sudden idea, and as William was speaking, James guided his pony toward Tim. Before he even spoke, Tim nodded and smiled his consent.

The others didn't object either. It took some time for William's gang to say their goodbyes and to get their packs readjusted. William carefully got his own supplies separated and onto his pinto mare, which he called Babe. The new trio watched as the other miners took off ahead of them.

Right away William looked over the younger men's two horses. After questioning Tim and James about their winter supplies, he did a quick inventory. "We should be able to make it all last a good couple of months before we start to run low. It'll do."

Of course, they were all optimistically hoping that would be all the time needed to get their gold. James and Tim were now eager and enthused to try mining under William's guidance.

"We'll do whatever you think best, brother," James said.

"Well, I've got more than a year's experience over you two, but only a small handful of gold to show for it. I hope I don't disappoint you with my own limited know-how." William explained that his earnings were back in the bank at Shasta City as the three of them took off toward the northern side of the Cottonwood Creek area.

They chattered cheerfully along the way as James caught William up with the family news. He quickly shared the best news from home since his brother had left close to two years earlier. "Elizabeth and I have a strong healthy son, born just about twenty months ago! We named him Charles Alva, after her brother and father."

William burst out, "I'm an uncle! I can hardly wait to see this little guy. Imagine a new little person in our family without me even knowing it," he mused and grew silent as they single-filed their horses up the hillside.

By the end of that same day, they settled in the spot William chose. It was close to a stream he said looked promising. Some big fir trees provided shelter for their tents. Tim and James shared their tent just as planned. William set up his own tent next to theirs but on the side closer to the creek.

The next day the three started into a routine that they repeated daily. They all rose at sunrise, ate a cold breakfast, worked the creek, took a brief noonday break, and worked until dark. Then they took turns cooking a hot meal for all. There was such a relaxing afternoon warmth, James often snuck in an afternoon nap. The high sun warmed him, making it too hard for him to resist.

They steadily panned, dug, and scrounged for golden pieces or any tiny flecks. But few were found.

At the end of their sixth day, William shouted, "I found some glitter over here!" Hurrying over to William, James's own eyes confirmed that he'd actually discovered a few tiny flecks. However, as hard as they worked that spot over the next two days, no more was found. After the initial excitement, the lack of any more findings for the next week weighed heavily on them all.

This was a higher elevation than James and Tim had ever wintered at before, and the constant chill and lack of success eventually dampened their adventuresome spirits. The chilly temperature turned freezing, but they still struggled on working the icy creeks using their cradle and picks through the next month.

Day by day, James watched Tim's optimism fade. Turning more and more inward as he worked, Tim rarely whistled anymore and spoke only when needed. When he did actually speak out, he griped about the weather, the food, or their bad luck.

With growing concern, William and James looked at each other with serious eyes whenever Tim started to gripe. They both found it hard to know what to say or how to help Tim.

James's concern grew into the tough realization that this wasn't the same man he'd known for so many years. Eventually, during one of their accustomed midday rests, he broached the subject with Tim. "I hate to see you so despondent, my friend. Can you tell me what you're thinking? Do you have it in ya to last here all winter?"

Tim's brooding eyes looked up, and James glimpsed his despair. Wondering if Tim was even going to reply, James held his gaze with a new resolve to help his dear friend.

Finally, Tim's lips moved slowly to form words. "Well, I've been thinking some 'bout moving on elsewhere. I don't think I can take more of this cold or this no-good work." Silence followed again. James didn't know what to say.

Tim went on, "But, James, it pains me to leave as good a friend as you've been to me. It hurts deeply to think about separating from our partnership. My hopes for a rich future have driven me hard for the past year. Now I don't even know if I even have any future left out here in these western parts. As hard as we've tried, I'm 'bout ready to admit defeat, James. I keep hoping the next day..." Tim trailed off weakly.

After quietly thinking about those words, James gave him an understanding back slap then held him by both shoulders. Locking his eyes with Tim's, in a wavering voice he replied, "Be assured that departing from here won't mean anything has come between us. It just means that God has a different path for you now. I can be satisfied with that. You aren't yourself in this place here, so I see you need to do something about that."

And with that, they could finally talk openly about their doubts and discouragement. Soon Tim decided he was going to go farther south, hoping for warmer weather. Feeling a little more optimistic once again, he also hoped for better gold fields.

Now forced to consider his own options, James didn't feel he was done here. He really wanted to keep pursuing this claim with William, who was stubbornly determined to stay through the winter. Plus, knowing he couldn't desert his brother without family guilt haunting him helped James decide to stick it out in this place.

The next day, James watched Tim pack up and helped him with the food he'd need. When Tim was done, he turned to James. Neither of them knew what to say. James broke the awkward silence first. "I will miss you fiercely. I only have good wishes and prayers for God's best for you, dear friend. You'd better keep in touch somehow."

Tim was finding it hard to speak at all, and he gave James a long, silent embrace. Pulling away, he finally said, "I will do that."

Mounting his cayuse, Tim turned and headed back to Shasta City.

Chapter 13

Despite his assuring words to Tim, the suddenness of their separation sent self-doubts tumbling through James like he'd never experienced since leaving Missouri. The loss of his friend caused something in his own hopes to start drying up. James began to inwardly question all his recent decisions.

He muttered aloud, "Who was I trying to fool? Me, a gold miner! How did I ever get to this place? What a dreamer. I've really been just a disillusioned farmer and dreaming of an easier life. Only fools like me were lured into this gold-seeking business. The wiser men are still at home with their family's love, comfort, and support." With these thoughts, he tumbled off deeper into his mighty misgivings like a rock rolling down a steep cliff. Tim's departure had given him the initial push.

James started struggling daily with these self-doubts and found no pleasure in the beauty of his surroundings or the tasks at hand. He miserably plodded through the motions of digging and moving the freezing dirt and rocks. Even when there were some successes in their search, he couldn't get excited by the golden flecks or even the small stones they managed to find. Supper times became much quieter between the brothers. James usually ignored William's attempts to cheer him up. Occasionally James gave him a pitiful, weak smile and response.

"James, you've got a start on your gold collection now. I know it's been tough and slow, but you've got a start," William said encouragingly.

"Yeah, I know you're right, Will. It's just so much slower than I'd ever expected. I'm struggling with a deep loneliness for Elizabeth and Charles that's set in along with such slow going," James replied.

Only William could see the irony between his brother's recent assurances to Tim and now James's own situation. Surely William couldn't help but be confused by James's duplicity. James's self-doubting led on to more days like this. The cold air, instead of being bracing and refreshing as it had been a few weeks previously, now sucked the energy out of him. The storm clouds moved in, and he felt them deep in his soul. The severity of the weather definitely matched James's mood.

One day after a sudden hailstorm, both brothers stepped out from their shelter to survey the damage to the combination of tent and wooden shack they called home. The east side was damaged the most, as the canvas had already been frayed and was now clearly ripped more than two feet high.

Taking charge like he always needed to lately, William spoke. "We're going to have to go into Shasta for a canvas patch now. Along with that we could certainly use some more food staples. I'm getting tired of potatoes and carrots, aren't you?" This was his slim disguise in hopes a change of scenery would help James's spirits.

James didn't argue. "It'd probably be good for you to get around some other people and sights, William. I know I'm sorry company for you."

Before long James was silently pondering just taking off from Shasta City and heading back home to Elizabeth. He'd return home with little money and mostly defeated, but alive and healthy, at least. Hopefully, he could get his crop farm back to profiting. The years of extremely hard winters back in Adair County had to change, he surmised. Even if they didn't, he might as well be there, cold and hungry but surrounded by family, rather than out here, cold and hungry with only William.

Making his decision to just give it up and go home brought him some relief. He finally slept a whole night through.

As the cold from a dead fire stirred his morning consciousness, he rose from his warm cot to get the fire started again. Standing, shivering, and reaching for the dry kindling they kept inside, he suddenly remembered last night's decision to pack it up and head back home. Just that thought warmed him! He would break the news gently to William as soon as he woke up.

The crackling of the kindling sounded cheerful as he stoked it. After using all the kindling kept inside, he pushed open the tent flap to retrieve some more. They kept the rest of their firewood stacked out on the driest side of the tent. Abruptly, James stopped short as snow slid down the canvas door and some fell onto his bare head. Shaking and clearing snow off his face and head, he squinted out at the brightness. More than ten inches of snow had fallen during the night while he had slept so soundly!

Chapter 14

At the noise, William rose and came to see what had startled James. He too just stared at the newly fallen snow. It didn't take long for each of them to realize their trip to Shasta City was postponed that day. And so it was the next day, and the next. Within those three days, they had a total of nearly two feet of new snow. As much as James usually enjoyed the first snowfall of winter, this snow had become his adversary. His hopes of soon starting his return trip back home wavered daily according to the weather.

On the fourth day, a day after the snows had stopped, William and he started talking again about that supply trip into Shasta. Their supplies were so low that trekking out and breaking a trail through the snow seemed to be the only option. They began ambitious plans to leave the next day.

Sensing the time was now, James shared his new plan with his brother. "William, I may not be coming back here with you after we get into Shasta City. I'm more homesick than I ever imagined and can only think about getting back home."

William desperately responded, "The winters aren't as long here as they are back home. We'll be able to get outside soon and go at it harder than ever. We can try a new creek or go wherever you'd like best. Our luck is going to change. I just know we are so close to it—our biggest find ever!"

What an optimist, James thought. A part of him wanted to believe William, but mostly he'd just had enough and was still determined to get home. "I've made up my mind, William. You're more cut out for this than I am. Your spirit doesn't give up. Mine gave up weeks ago."

When William finally accepted James's decision, they continued their plans to start out the following day, before the weather turned on them again.

Rising first the next morning, James built only a small fire, since they'd be moving out soon. He did want to remember to bring in more firewood to keep dry for William while they were gone. Grabbing a few smaller logs, he set them off to his side of the tent. That might help him remember to do that later, he hoped. As James got busy packing to really leave here, William rose and started breakfast. He was able to cook over the snapping fire that was set under their small smoke pipe. As the tent started its regular steaming process, James knew he wouldn't ever miss this smell of damp canvas mixed with smoke.

Tense with excitement about getting out of there and starting homeward, James ate and got his bedding packed up. Next they tackled securing the tent against any strong winds while they were gone. And he remembered to bring in some more firewood for William. William still stubbornly planned to try this same creek some more.

They loaded mostly empty bags onto his pony and William's mare and took off downhill. They slowly crossed the icy fields by midmorning, trying to guide their horses carefully enough not to injure their legs in the broken ice. As the sun got higher, so did their spirits. James was eagerly looking forward to cashing in his two gold rocks and bag of gold flecks. He would then symbolically be getting gold out of his system. Slowly and cautiously, they led the animals more often than rode them. Moving at this slow, unsure pace for a few hours, they anticipated coming soon upon the largest of several streams on their route. It'd be a perfect spot to water, feed, and take a short rest.

With his excitement still high, James was silently praising God for the sparkling beauty everywhere around him. However, his inner revelry was interrupted by an unexpected and increasingly loud roar coming from a crevice over to the west. Approaching the area with apprehension, he reached the crest and soon spotted the cause of the clamor. Astonishingly, the stream was rolling at twice its height since they last crossed it in October.

William quietly pulled his mule up beside James. They both stared, silently processing what lay before them. When his eyes registered what he was seeing with his brain, James's excitement died like the last ember of their campfire must have died that morning.

In disappointment, he turned to look at his brother and impatiently asked, "Have you heard of any other crossings we could use? Others must have gotten out in conditions like this before. What did they do?" He stopped, knowing his questions were futile, as poor William probably didn't know any more than he did. He'd only been here one winter ahead of James, and he would've already spoken up if he had any answers.

They took a rest break in mostly silence to eat and then feed their stock. James finally broke the silence, with a grudging, "I guess you've got me for a partner awhile longer. If I'm going to be stuck here, at least it's with you, William."

William acknowledged that with a smile and said, "My condolences, brother. I do believe you are stuck with me. That being, I'm proposing we look for some of the other campers farther up Cottonwood Creek and see what they're doing for supplies."

That made more sense than just turning back, so they loaded up again and started back toward the northeast. There they hoped to connect with the other group William had mined with formerly or another pair of men that had passed their camp back in the fall. William thought his friends would be about eight miles away, so they started back to the northeast.

William was right. By nightfall they had found the group. They were greeted warmly and encouraged to stay there, so James and William camped nearby.

For the next few months, all the streams continued to be extremely high. It became almost impossible for anyone to go out for provisions or anyone to bring them in. At times, it looked as though they might all starve. They'd found a third group of stranded miners. The collection of food among all the groups amounted in the last sack of flour being divided out at $1.12 per pound, and a half-starved cow at 40 cents per pound. A man named Peter, who went by the name of "Long Kentuck," had raised a small crop of corn the year before, which he sold at 38 cents per pound. Dried apples were cheap and plentiful among the group, so between corn and apples, the two brothers got through the winter.

The days crept by. They spent the rest of the month involved in just meeting their basic survival needs. The few things James enjoyed were looking for fallen trees and branches and chopping them up for firewood, tending the fire, and talking about back home with William. Now and then, he was struck by the beauty of the sun's sparkle off an icy tree or a moonlight scene on snowy meadows. Mostly he longed for the embrace of his family, though.

As he was going from lethargy to impatience on a weekly cycle, James approached William one day. "I just have to see if the creek has subsided any yet. Let's take the half-day trek out and check again. It's been over two weeks. It could be down."

William replied, "Since I know you're so anxious, I can oblige you. I'd enjoy the change of scenery, even if it's a wasted trip and we just have to turn around again."

They rode off the next sunny morning, and James moved with high hopes. William observed his brother's energetic behavior and spoke up as they covered the first mile. "Now, you know, James, it's most likely the creek's still swollen. I advise you to enjoy this trip outdoors we're making together, but don't hope for more. That way you won't be so disappointed."

"I know you're trying to caution me and protect me, big brother. Still, I've just got to keep hoping I can get out of here and head back home soon. I'm praying that God has mercy on my anxious soul. I'm trusting Him with this trip today."

William was right to caution James, for when they approached the stream, the rushing noise and sight of the creek stopped them both in their tracks. James was the first to move. He grabbed his hat off his head and hit his leg with it. He wailed, "Nooo!" He jumped off his horse and paced along the marshy creek bank muttering, "No, no, no! Lord, I can't believe this. I think I've waited long enough."

After getting his boots wet pacing the shore, he stopped and looked up at William. "I really appreciate that you came out here this far with me. You probably knew that I had to see it for myself. I appreciate you letting me come and look."

William had pity on his brother and didn't say much. They fed their horses and then turned back, both of them discouraged. They arrived back at camp the very same day. They were both resigned now to continue waiting out the winter weather.

Chapter 15

It seemed that just as they resigned themselves to wait out the winter, suddenly spring opened in February. They were in the most beautiful country James had ever seen. After their severe winter, he would never have dreamed he'd enjoy this place like he did. The air felt pleasantly fresh and warm, and within two weeks, the face of the earth was fairly covered with flowers.

Over the months they'd been snowed in, James had figured out what money he needed to get back east. He was planning to go back by steamship. Some of the other miners had convinced him it was the fastest way back home.

In the pleasant weather and beautiful countryside, William persuaded James to try mining with him a little while longer. James agreed, since he knew he'd better earn some more funds to get him back across the country. So he willingly postponed his trip awhile in hopes of finding some gold.

They actually did much better mining the next two months of spring. Together William and James found several nuggets of gold weighing an ounce or more, one of which weighed about six ounces. William spoke encouragingly to James, "I'd say that one nugget is worth about $118!" Finally feeling encouraged for his efforts, James was actually enjoying his mining experience. He found it was easy to keep postponing his return trip a few more weeks. Getting as much gold as he could while it was going well continued to motivate him.

As fast as the winter had hit them, it was that fast that the spring rains stopped and the streams dried up. It seemed like one April day they were successfully running their placer mine along their best stream, and then the next day that same stream quickly dried down to a trickle. They watched in dismay as it dried up completely within a week. Each of those seven days, they discussed possible new ideas and ventures they could try.

However, being personally satisfied, James kept telling William he was ready to leave toward the nearest seaport and get a ship back home. That port would probably be San Francisco, from what he'd been told. William's only future plan was more mining elsewhere. So they ended their camp there, packed the animals, and set out for their long-anticipated separation. They also divided all the gold in two parts.

James grieved on the day they actually parted and William left him to go mining up the Sacramento River on his own. Not knowing when or if they'd see each other again was especially painful. Neither had received any more news from home. That made James wonder when he'd see any of his family again and compounded the grief he felt.

He turned his own pony toward Shasta City, planning to exchange his gold and get on south as fast as he could. In Shasta City, he still didn't find any letters from home. He banked his gold, stabled his horse, ate up, and refreshed there until early May. He was making plans for his return trip by ship when instead of heading south, he was talked into a new mining adventure.

Chapter 16

Elizabeth

The departing Bushnells soon joined up with many others from around the county, and by mid-April they were on their way to Oregon. They chose to become a part of a group headed by Captain Vincent McClure and his brother Lieutenant James McClure. These men had a guidebook and much advice from previous travelers, which qualified them as good leaders in Jason's opinion.

The women fell into a pleasant enough routine of walking along the wagons and visiting as they watched all their children old enough to walk by their sides. Charles Alva was too young to walk much, so Elizabeth mostly only got to stretch her legs and visit with others when he was napping in the wagon. She was very grateful he still took two good naps daily. That broke the routine up nicely for her.

Elizabeth was certainly glad she had both strong brothers-in-law along. They'd soon learned that one man was needed for driving or leading the wagon while the other took care of guiding their spare teams of oxen and cow. The men took turns at these jobs. Her mother-in-law was very helpful with all the daily setting up, cooking, and then packing up that came with constantly camping in new spots most every day along the trail. Elizabeth enjoyed watching Mother Bushnell care for baby

Charles too. Mother and the baby were developing their own special relationship. With all of her family helping, Elizabeth enjoyed the change after being alone so much over the past year.

In the next few months of traveling, they crossed the monstrous grassy plains and trekked through the late snow of the Rocky Mountains. The captains declared often that they were making good time. Then, right after they passed the most magnificent waterfalls she'd ever seen and they were actually on the edge of the Oregon Territory, things changed—at least for her family and 250 other wagons. At that spot toward the end of August, they made a decision that greatly altered their course.

Chapter 17

A Mr. Elijah Elliott met the Bushnells' wagon train at Fort Boise, the eastern edge of the Oregon Country. Jason heard that he'd come from the mid-Willamette Valley to meet up with his wife and children, who were on their same wagon train. His family was finally being reunited here in Fort Boise. Mr. Elliott had property in the middle Willamette Valley at a place called Pleasant Hill, and he was a representative sent by a group of settlers from there. Those settlers were hoping to find some willing emigrants that would try the new, free road that Elliott and his neighbors had built.

While everyone was resting themselves at the fort, caring for their stock, replenishing supplies, and repairing wagons after the mountain crossing, Mr. Elliott talked to all the men he could, especially the captains in the train. Mr. Elliott proposed, "We've got a new road being built from the middle Willamette Valley out to here, and it's almost done. I'd like to lead some of your trains departing for the southwest from here. We'll get to the best, flattest, and most fertile land in the whole Willamette Valley! We'd separate from the main trail here and head south to meet up with the new road. It's 130 miles shorter, and it'll save you weeks of travel. That will help you get to claim some of the best farmlands ahead of the others."

It seemed to Elizabeth, by looking around her, that most families in their large group wanted to enjoy Fort Boise longer. That evening she heard Mrs. Nelson say, "After we rest and stock up here, I hope we can hurry along north and get to an even bigger fort I've heard about. That Fort Dalles is on the Columbia River, and it means we're almost there. I think it's the biggest fort we're going to see, and supposedly they're very helpful to all the emigrants coming through. I'll feel so relieved once we get that far, knowing we're almost to the valley."

Mrs. Nelson had captured the other women's attention and hopes too. Elizabeth was interested in seeing the mighty Columbia River. She'd already heard so much about the river's beauty and magnificence from trappers and traders at each post along the way, she was anxious to see it. And to hear that this wonderful-sounding Fort Dalles sat along that river made that northern route sound just fine to Elizabeth.

However, Jason and Cory said Captain McClure and some of the men were seriously considering using Elliott's proposed faster route to the Willamette Valley. Some had read about Samuel Meek's new route to the south. It had been a successful shortcut for most of the wagon trains that followed Meek. Captain McClure admitted he knew about one train that had gotten lost last year, but he assured them that wisdom had surely been gained from that mishap. It certainly wouldn't happen again.

Since James had talked to all his family about heading toward the Willamette Valley and even farther south on his gold mining route, Elliott's new plan held definite interest for Jason and Cory. All of them, including Elizabeth, could see at this point in their travels that going there made some sense. She just wished they didn't have to be leaving the security of the proven traditional trail others were taking.

Due to Mr. Elliott's confidence and enthusiasm, all the Bushnells, Captain James McClure's family, and quite a few other families were convinced to follow Elliott's route. This meant that their new group of a hundred wagons left from Fort Boise and headed south the very next day. Elizabeth was surprised to see that within a week many others joined up with them; soon they totaled 250 wagons, all attempting the new road. With these additional folks along, their excitement grew at the prospects ahead. Even the upset women, disturbed about leaving the main trail, became more optimistic as they headed off toward the southwest.

Within that first week, they left the forests and mountains of northeastern Oregon behind them. Mr. Elliott and Captain McClure led them, still following the traditional Oregon Trail up to the point where it crossed the Malheur River. It was here they turned west to follow their new route, which started to disturb Elizabeth. She'd suddenly realized they had departed from the route James had talked so much about. His "trail talk" had almost made it seem familiar to her. Now, James's own family was leaving that path to follow another advised by a perfect stranger.

Well, she told herself, *even James claimed often enough that the Willamette Valley had the best farmland.* She reassured herself that this new trail was going to get them more easily and quickly to wherever James might be. She prayed over her uneasiness and left it in God's hands. Besides God, she just hoped James would approve of their new decision.

Chapter 18

James

James ran into his friend Peter, the one who they called Long Kentuck. His friend, too, had left his winter and spring camp and was regrouping in Shasta. It was he who did the convincing for James to start another mining adventure.

"James," exclaimed Long Kentuck, "I've just heard the best news about some brand-new mines on the Pitt River. That's just two days from here. Go with me! Let's get in on these fresh mines!"

"Naw, I'm ready to go back to my wife and son in Missouri. I've been gone too long already. I've got my profits I made with William, and I really need to get heading back home."

Kentuck's enthusiasm over these newly discovered mines on the Pitt and its tributary, Squaw Creek, was contagious, though. "This may be the best gold streak around here anybody's ever seen. James, it won't take very long to get you some more gold for your big trip. We could get going over there, start to work, and quickly find out for sure."

James looked silently over at the hills Kentuck pointed toward for a few moments. "All right, you've got me intrigued. I'll go with you up Squaw Creek for a trial of one week," James agreed.

Away the two men went the next day with their fresh supplies and fresh outlook. They arrived along the Pitt River on their second day, but they continued on to the small, rocky creek running along it before stopping. Their horses easily stuck their noses into the rippling waters there as the men smoothed out a large camp area along the rocky beach. The camp included room for their work spot, where James easily set up their dry mine.

Then the next day, they began their new pattern of working from sunup to noon without a break, then they took their refreshment hour, after which they worked again until dark. They weren't working the creek since Kentuck had been told that the most promise was in the rock outcroppings heading away from the creek. They set up their dry mines, or placer mines, which required digging in and through the rocks. A streak of quartz was the clue to gold nearby, and that's what they hoped to find among these rocks around them.

Their routine was to always head out in opposite directions and work back toward each other. On the third day of his picking and digging back toward Kentuck, James saw a glitter that made his heart jump. Yes! Sure enough, as he kept swinging a few more strokes, his pick struck a small quartz vein on the hillside. This quartz line grew and soon led him to gold streaks with the vein.

This vein turned out good enough that James and Kentuck together took out about four hundred dollars' worth to share. That was enough encouragement to keep them both mining in that spot five days longer.

When this mine started to dwindle, James decided it was time to move on toward home again. They decided that he'd leave Long Kentuck there in that spot, as his friend was content to stay and search further. With a grateful heart, James said his goodbye, and he and his pony turned once more to Shasta City.

Just over two weeks before, he'd left on deposit with Wells Fargo & Co. back in Shasta City the previous gold he'd gotten during the long, hard winter and beautiful early spring with William. With each mile closer to that city, James became increasingly anxious to collect his gold and get on home with it. He occupied the miles of the trip with daydreams of their new life—Elizabeth, little Charles, and him. These pleasant thoughts kept him company as Cayuse and he traveled along toward the south.

Excitedly, James coaxed the pony up to the top of their final hill. He was eager to glimpse a view of the town of Shasta. Apparently, Cayuse wasn't nearly as excited, as the pony began halting and resisting James's lead.

"Now, there, Cayuse. We need to keep moving forward," James coaxed and prodded. "Whatever's gotten into you? No, we're not stopping here!"

Now James smelled wafts of smoke drifting toward them. He figured this must be causing his pony's strange actions. At the ridge, he gazed in disbelief. His eyes could find nothing left of the city but for a half dozen huts on the former outskirts. The rest of town, which had been mostly canvas-covered houses, was now just smoking ruins.

Moving slowly down the ridge, he had to be very firm handed to keep Cayuse moving forward. The smoke was thicker as they approached. James's eyes burned as he rapidly took in the tragedy. His heart sank as he realized that his gold, kept in a buckskin purse, was a part of that fire too.

It appeared to have been a very recent fire. As he neared the first outskirts, a woman answered his questions.

"The whole town burned up just last night," she said. "No one has said yet how or where it started. Most people spent the night watching the remaining slow burn. Some tried to sleep in those makeshift camps. Now, some are out looking around for anything left. Others are just deciding to move on as soon as possible."

After thanking her, James with fear and dread kept his pony moving toward the smoldering ruins. The citizens who were camped outside the rubble quietly watched him ride past. They looked shocked and depressed. It was eerily still. Even dogs and children stood looking confused at the piles of ashes and reeking smoke. In these hushed surroundings, he stopped Cayuse and dismounted. Looking for where to start his own search among the hot ashes, he aimed for where he thought the bank had stood.

A few others were looking and poking through the rubble, and one middle-aged man greeted him. "I've been at it since sunup, and I've had to wait for most places to cool down before I can even get close. Let me show you the hottest areas, those that are still too hot to search through. By the way, what will you be looking for?"

James replied, "I had my gold in the Wells Fargo Bank. I'm thinking it was about over here," he said as he pointed to the general area ahead of him.

This helpful stranger said, "Yep, that's about as good as I could guess too. Stay away from that side to your right, though, as it is too hot to walk anywhere near there yet. Also, farther up there beside that pile of scorched bricks is way too hot to approach. You'll see embers still smoldering if you get any nearer."

Misery does love company, James thought as he was encouraged by this sad-looking man. James said, "Thank you kindly for your help, and I pray you will find some of your own belongings soon."

Using the stick he'd picked up back on the edge of town, James poked and pushed around the closest debris. Praying silently as he searched, he kept at it for thirty to forty minutes. Then he changed his direction over to one of the hotter areas he'd been warned about. Cautiously moving in closer and closer, scooting aside piles of soft ashes, he poked and prodded along. It was in the edge of some of these warmer ashes that his stick hit something small but hard. The size of it started his heart beating a little faster.

Excitedly, he kept digging and soon uncovered a set of keys, brass keys like from a business—maybe a bank? Swinging them up out of the ashes, he hollered for the bank owner. Not that he knew for sure if the banker was even there among the few searchers; he was just hoping. A grimy but friendly face approached, and James trustingly turned over this treasure, never actually knowing if that was truly the banker under all that dirt. However, he wanted to believe he was near the bank.

Returning to that same smoldering area, James prodded some more. In the next few minutes, his stick hit a soft lump. Upon more scraping, it looked like a buckskin bag. He swung it up off the warm coals, and it did appear to be a buckskin purse—just like his buckskin purse. It was burned to a crisp but not broken. Hoping this was really his, he cleared a spot on the ground with his boot and dumped out everything in the bag. There was his gold still unharmed! Giddy with joy, he danced in a circle as he joyfully blew off the ash and looked at the gold. Happily he said, "Thank you, thank you, Almighty God," loudly enough for anyone to hear.

Feeling very generous after such good fortune, he stayed in Shasta another day to help others in their searches for surviving possessions. Camping near some local fellows that night, he heard them surmise that the fire had started in the livery stable. The blacksmith had died in the fire, so they'd never know what happened. Within that next twenty-four hours, most had either found something valuable or had given up on ever seeing their possessions again. Despite his sympathies for the townsfolk, it was time for him to move on again.

Chapter 19

Still having heard nothing from Elizabeth or his mother and brothers, James started down the valley back toward the town of Cottonwood. Traveling mostly downhill and following the Sacramento River south, he and Cayuse wound over much unbroken terrain. It was a tragic day when Cayuse turned his leg on a rough, rocky patch of trail. James stopped to clean the pony's broken leg and wrap a stick splint with a torn shirt around it. After three days of leading the horse, he sorrowed as the leg refused to heal properly. The pony's strength was giving out. It was a tiring trip, and James's food supplies were very sparse, and the burned town of Shasta hadn't helped. He survived a few more days of traveling on apples and old bread.

A few long, weary days later, he approached the Cottonwood community. Going to the livery stable first, James was forced to retire his pony, Cayuse, who had served him so well. Mr. Smith from the livery offered a few dollars for the injured animal. James took it without asking the fate of his trusty pony, as that was more than he wanted to think about. Even though James wanted to leave Mr. Smith as soon as he got his money, he quickly thought to ask, "Where does a stranger go for some good food and a room to rent here?"

Mr. Smith replied, "There's a boarding house run by the Ericsons that I recommend. They're good, clean, honest folks."

James found the Ericsons' boarding house a few streets over and was welcomed there. After being shown his single room, the first thing he did was accept their offer of a bath. Mr. Ericson and his son each carried in two bucketsful of heated water apiece. James soaked and relaxed in the warmed water. When he was dressed and feeling civil again, he went down to the dinner table. He ate a delicious meal with the other four boarders. Besides enjoying the good cooking, he got caught up on some of the news around the region and a little beyond California.

James was disappointed to learn that the steamships heading back east were not as regular as he'd hoped. According to the men around the table, the next ship leaving San Francisco for the Panama country was his fastest route east. However, a ship wouldn't be departing for almost another whole month.

James visited in the parlor until he could hardly keep his eyes open. Fearing he was being impolite, he excused himself and headed for his room. Before he could contemplate all this news and what his next move would be, he fell sound asleep.

In the morning, James remembered the ship's schedule and that disturbing news. He was stuck trying to figure out what he'd do for the next month. Soon, he heard at breakfast that an itinerant preacher had come into the community. The preacher had caused a big stir, and the news traveled quickly through the neighborhood.

Marveling at this good fortune, James stayed there another night and enjoyed a church service held right in the parlor of the Ericsons' boarding house. He was delighted to be able to join in a worship service way out here in a tiny western burg.

Between finding his burned bag of gold and this church service suddenly appearing, James's spirits lifted knowing anew that God was with him. He would trust God with the long delay to catch a ship back east, too.

The next day being a Monday, James believed God must have been directing his steps again, as a rancher knocked on the door of the boarding house while they breakfasted. The rancher, a Mr. Wagner, was looking for harvesters he could hire for a few weeks out on his ranch. Feeling so led by a sovereign God recently, James took this as another divine opportunity and agreed to hire out with Wagner. Gathering his few bags, James thanked his hosts for their kindness, paid them their due, and left for the six-mile ride out to the Wagner ranch.

Mr. Wagner had three hundred acres of mostly barley crops with only his two sons to assist him at the time. Now, along with two other hired men, James ended up harvesting with the Wagners, eating with them, and bedding in their barn for the next three weeks. He found it was a very comfortable situation compared to his recent mining camps.

Harvesting the barley was an unfamiliar experience for James. This was a new crop to him, and it taught him a few things about farming here that he was grateful to learn. For one thing, it took James very little time to realize how important it was to keep his shirt on while working in barley. Tom Wagner, the eldest son, had told them to keep their shirts on, but in the warm June weather, James forgot that advice—but only once.

"Yeow! These stalks are razor sharp!" barebacked James yelled to no one in particular but to whoever was near. Trying to avoid the sharp stalks, called "awns," from then on, he was able to work a few rows before his skin started to itch and redden.

"What is going on here?" said James to his neighbor harvester.

This man, only known to James as Gus, explained, "I know some men get skin irritations from this plant, but not everyone. Sorry to see you're one of them that do."

James went and grabbed the shirt he'd left a few rows back and put it on. He continued trying to work with his itchy skin plaguing him. He wasn't relieved until that evening, when he could apply the baking soda and cold water he was given. Thankfully, he could get to sleep, and he was fine the next day. He learned quickly to never take his shirt off in barley fields again, no matter how hot he got!

He helped with this late May crop and was amazed to hear that it would be replanted again once this harvest was done. Then it would be harvested again in the fall. It was called a biannual crop; that was unheard of to James.

Mr. Wagner used his barley for fattening up his cattle and swine then sold his excess to other farmers for the same use. One night there was some talk around supper of another use for barley. The younger men heard of a fellow known to be using barley to produce a malt that helped in brewing beer. Apparently, none of Wagner's men had seen this done successfully out here in California. James could tell that these men didn't have any interest in putting their time or money into experimenting with beer production. James agreed with their decision. Not many folks out west had resources to spend on creating such a luxury item.

The rhythm of the harvest work made time pass quickly, and nearly a month expired. At the end of his month in Cottonwood, James had acquired a total of $50. The harvest was done. James was satisfied and ready to start off again for San

Francisco. He said in parting with Mr. Wagner, "I am very obliged for the work, your hospitality, and all that I've learned from you and your sons. May God keep your family all safe and with good health. I'm off to be reunited with my own dear family." And with that, he was off again toward the south.

Chapter 20

Footing it from the Wagners' farm on down to Red Bluff, James found a side-wheeler ship bound for Sacramento. He paid for his passage and was soon on board. His departing view from the water in this luscious country was inspiring. Riding on the Sacramento River, although it was much smaller than the Mississippi, was a delight to his eyes and a rest to his body. He enjoyed letting the river do all the work for a while.

Back on land in Sacramento, he stayed overnight in the town. It was a big enough town to have pharmacies, attorney firms, brass foundries, and other shops. He could see that fresh fish were being sold in several places, as the city sat at the confluence of the American and Sacramento Rivers. The thought of eating some fish made James's mouth water.

James ate a fish dinner and spent that night there, but he was anxious to keep going down to San Francisco. Taking off on another paddle ship larger than his last, he arrived in San Francisco the next day, which was the last day of June, 1853.

At this time the city of San Francisco was headquarters for all the gamblers and toughs from the mines. A rough population was growing quickly here. A good part of the town was built on piles over the water, James observed. Living on boards over the water made sense to these types of men, James thought—

men looking for quick money and not caring to put down any roots.

Not liking the kind of men he encountered here, James was very glad when he and all his gold took safe passage on the steamship *Sierra Nevada* within two days. The ship was heading for San Juan, the western terminus of the Nicaragua ship route, and he was ecstatic to be finally heading home! That is, until the ship passed out of the Golden Gate and the first ocean wave struck.

Chapter 21

James soon realized that neither walking up on deck, standing still, nor sitting would help him get through his extreme seasickness. Confined to lying in his berth, he resigned himself to the regular use of a bucket provided by a sympathetic crew member. In his second day of confinement, James caught a heavy chill from the draftiness of the ship's lower deck. While trying to get to the water tank on the third day, he fainted and fell hard to the floor. Some of the men who were gathered around the water tank picked him up and carried his weak body back to his berth.

The next morning, James went to the ship's doctor for some medical help. For a remedy, James was unknowingly given a big dose of calomel. The doctor prescribed and used it as a purgative, which James didn't need as his stomach was completely empty. With a sore burned mouth and throat, he couldn't swallow any solid food for several days. His stomach ailments were now combined with these other extremely painful problems. He was miserable.

He prayed, *Lord, I don't know how much more of this I can take. Heal my mouth and help me get my strength back. I need your help forgiving that no-good doctor too. He didn't even take the time to listen to my symptoms.*

Just like an answer to his prayer, as soon as he opened his eyes, a man on the opposite berth mercifully brought him a big drink of water. This wise man realized that James was badly dehydrated. That act of kindness in a drink of water was the turning point in his recovery.

Once recovered from the doctor's mistreatment of calomel, James found his sea legs in about four or five days. He could finally walk on the deck and visit with other passengers. The ship was full of returning miners, between seven and eight hundred altogether. He enjoyed the warm tropical breezes that picked up every late afternoon and evening. He found the cook's food tasty enough now that he could eat it and keep it down.

The ship reached Acapulco, in Mexico, eight days out. There was a newly built seaport, as the original town had been burned down by the Spanish during the Mexican War of Independence. James's only view of this major transport city was from his ship; only the crew was allowed on shore to replenish supplies. They set sail the very next morning, and James watched Mexico disappear.

After five more days of calm sailing, they reached San Juan. It was July of 1853. The passengers' excitement over reaching the San Juan port was balanced by the fact that there were no facilities there for landing. The few women of their party were landed by small boats onto a big rock as all the men watched apprehensively from the deck.

When it was the men's turn, they were rowed to within a few rods of the shore, where the water was three or four feet deep. Three small boats were used over and over again to get all the men to shore. Here stood a swarm of naked natives to meet them, each one eager to earn a quarter by carrying a passenger ashore. They cried out in English to the passengers, "Pick a back!" With his baggage in his hands, James jumped astride a big, strong-looking Negro's neck and was safely carried ashore. For the rest of his life afterwards, whenever he heard the term "piggyback" he always remembered this ride.

Chapter 22

James was happy to be back on land after two weeks at sea. He and those of his companions traveling farther had to get to Nicaragua Lake, which was twelve miles away. The crew told them they could walk or hire a donkey from there. Choosing to ride on a thin but capable donkey, James joined the other riders following in a long string on a rocky, narrow road. Amid the jungle, he was able to admire this beautiful country. Everything here was growing in tropical profusion, with palm trees and thick vines often blocking out the light. Chattering monkeys, flashing parrots, and other beautiful birds filled the woods. Plantains and bananas were growing all around him. He was amazed that he could reach out and pick the fruit whenever he wanted.

The animals took them across many small streams, and James hung on loosely since he was impressed with his own surefooted donkey. Toward the end of the first day, much of their trail ran through swifter streams full of loose stones. Here he held on more tightly, burying his arms and shoulders into his donkey's neck. Just two riders up from James, an older man yelled out alarmingly as his donkey stumbled. All behind him gasped, stopping suddenly, and then looking to see if that donkey could right itself again. The animal was down on one knee; the old man was barely able to stay seated and not go over the animal's head. The determined animal slowly labored up from that knee and straightened up once more. *Ahh!* The relief of the old gentleman, and all behind him watching, was strong enough to be felt if not heard. There were cheers and then concerned inquiries regarding the older man's ability to carry on. He chose to just sit a spell. Within ten minutes he was ready, and he prodded his faithful donkey onward.

On the last day, they plodded on through swamps lined with decaying donkey carcasses. James hated to see it and avoided as much as he could by turning away from those sights and smells. Apparently there'd been other traveling accidents on this trail, but no native or guide seemed concerned enough to have mentioned that to James and the other riders. It made James wonder how many donkeys were needed to get men safely across this short overland trek. He didn't have anyone near enough to ask, and he soon decided that the carcasses lying around told him plenty.

Arriving that same long day at magnificent Nicaragua Lake, the largest lake in the lower Americas, James's group of twenty men and three women stayed all night at Virgin Bay. Their lodging was a large, old Spanish adobe home. They slept four men in a room, and the women were in their own quarters. It seemed very roomy compared to their recent ship quarters.

James enjoyed the meal of fresh fish mixed with coconut and all the rice they could eat. There were many different fruits served. He discovered that the mango, which was new to him, was better than most fruits he'd ever experienced. However, all the fruit was especially tasty to him since he'd left the Willamette Valley and its fresh fruit behind.

From this side of the huge Lake Nicaragua, they would

embark on a steamer heading for San Carlos. The next morning aboard the steamer, they crossed the magnificent lake, going seventy miles to its outlet into the San Juan River. They all marveled as their passage took them near the huge volcanic island in the middle of the lake. It was a smooth and lovely ride for all, and soon it would be even more appreciated.

Arriving safely and calmly at Fort San Carlos, they disembarked and changed to some smaller and narrower boats to continue downriver. James heard the natives refer to them as "bunga boats." Once launched, their bunga boat shot down the narrow and rapid current like an arrow. The startled passengers hung on to the sides of the narrow boats and tried to avoid the splashing amongst these rushing rapids as much as possible. Most of them, including James, got wet anyway.

When they reached the first tidewaters, it was apparent to James that they were going to arrive in San Carlos before nightfall. With the boat going much more slowly now in the tidewaters, James observed to a boat mate, "Look at all those old logs on the bars over there." He paused, then added, "My goodness, they're starting to move!"

The oarsman chuckled at the surprise on James's face. "The streams here are full of alligators. We must move very slowly, as they do."

James was entranced as he watched them; they really did move very little. He replied to his oarsman, "Be sure to not give them any reason to hurry over here. This boat is too small for me to feel very secure with all of them around us. Just keep it slow and steady."

When it became apparent that they had to land on shore and get out, one man pointed to a farther riverbank, saying, "Let's get over as far away from these alligators as we can."

Even after they'd gone as far away as they possibly could, they all still stepped very cautiously and slowly onto land.

"Now that's as close as I ever hope to come to any alligator in my life," James stated. "Still, it was fascinating," he mused, and many heartily agreed with both his statements.

Chapter 23

The timing of their arrival was perfect, as James was able to get onboard the steamship *Northern Light*, which was sailing for New York that very same night. This ship only sailed twice a month from San Carlos, so he rejoiced over his good fortune! He couldn't help but be very anxious to set sail for his home. Since the gold fever had struck, this clipper regularly sailed from San Francisco, around Cape Horn, and then all the way north up to Boston. Soon after boarding, he was pleased to hear the sailors claim that this was the fastest clipper ship ever built. James's excitement increased greatly now that he was on the steamer and heading back to his northeastern United States country.

Heading for home at a fast pace now, the ship and passengers passed within view of Havana's city lights the very next night. The sight of those lights further filled James with hopes of seeing his family again soon. He knew that Florida would be sighted sometime the next day. He was getting so much closer to home each day.

As he stood on the deck lost in these homesick thoughts, the ship encountered a terrific storm of hard rain with deafening thunder and lightning. Within a few minutes of the downpour's beginning, the loud cracking sound of splitting timber caught everyone's attention, and James watched splinters fall from one of the pole masts. He continued to watch the pieces of the pole hit the deck and slide into the water. Due to the lightning, the crew he crew soon ordered James and the others below deck to stay out of danger—and out of the crew's way. James found it very hard to sleep below deck. Some of his sleeplessness was caused by the loud and terrifying weather, but he also worried about the ship's ability to be steered without the top mast. Being so close to North America, he feared another delay.

The captain proved capable of maneuvering his ship, and they kept a steady pace the next few days and nights. The seas calmed as the storm abated and left them alone.

The *Northern Light* safely arrived at New York on July 25, 1853. James's journey from San Francisco had taken him twenty-three days, and he was in good health, even after the calomel episode back aboard the *Sierra Nevada*.

Disembarking with most of his fellow passengers, he unloaded his bag at a cheap hotel close to the docks. In a shop near Seventh Avenue, he got new clothes. He took them back to his shared room and generally cleaned himself up good, using a lukewarm bath, water pitcher, and a decent towel. Then he went strolling through the neighborhoods some more. He felt good to be in this city of New York, which he had heard so much of all his life. It felt like he was finally in a part of America he knew, and that felt very good after all his recent adventures.

The streets were much busier here than any place he'd ever experienced. As he crossed the hard dirt streets, he was forced to carefully look out for the trolley cars, step over their tracks, and watch for the many, many horses and some carriages. He'd stop every so often just to look up at the tall buildings, the tallest he'd ever seen. Looking so far up made him wonder how people didn't get dizzy working up there that high above the ground.

Later that same day, he found the newly established Central Park, which covered over seven hundred acres of downtown Manhattan. He walked along the southern and eastern edges of the park and marveled at a city using this much land as a place for both the rich and the poor to relax and enjoy. The parts he saw were all landscaped and lovely. He strolled from there back to his hotel, buying food from a market on the way. The smells were a mix of some familiar and some very strange; however, he enjoyed the taste and aroma of the meat and bread he chose. He washed it down with a Vernor's ginger ale bought from a street vendor. This new type of carbonated drink was surely a treat. It also seemed extravagant to a country farmer like him. Still, he enjoyed the amber color and bubbly sensation very much.

He only had the one day to see New York City. The very next day, James and a few others from his clipper found the Grand Central Train Station, and they all left for Chicago. While James was laid over in Toledo in route to Chicago, he slept alone in a real bed for the first time since leaving home over a year ago. It was the most uncomfortable night in all his time away. James was surprised to learn that he could enjoy the soft side of a board, the ground, and the snoring of roommates, but this feather bed was misery to him!

The group of travelers reached Chicago on July 30 at 2:00 p.m. To James's surprise, there were only two railroads that linked the city of Chicago to the rest of the country—the Michigan Central from Toledo and another that ran on the Illinois Central Line, which used a one-hundred-mile track to the new town of Peru on the Illinois River. James headed for Peru. Only a few years incorporated, Peru was the most northern port on the Illinois River. There, he left the railroad behind him and found a steamboat passage down the Illinois River to St. Louis. He arrived in St. Louis having left Chicago four days earlier.

Now extremely anxious to reach home, he didn't spend any time enjoying St. Louis. Instead, James switched steamboats and departed the next morning on the mighty Mississippi River up to La Grange. From there, he took a stagecoach on to Adair County, and from the stage stop, he left for home on foot. As he walked, his anticipation was great and growing by the mile, but he still didn't know how great a surprise was waiting for him at home.

Chapter 24

By walking as quickly as possible, James reached a few neighboring farms just after dark. He was suddenly unsure where to go first. He was torn between getting to his own farm two miles farther on or stopping at his nearest relative's first. James stopped to think. Dirty and hungry, he decided to head to the nearest place first, which belonged to his sister, Helen, and brother-in-law, Frank Adkins. He planned on a quick cleanup and hopefully some food before rushing off to see his own precious family.

James turned down the familiar lane and soon met up with Frank, who was swinging an empty bucket and striding between the barn and his house. "Hello, Frank. It's me, James, back from the west."

Frank stopped suddenly and replied, "Well, I can't believe my eyes, but your voice convinces me it's really you, James! What a welcome surprise!" He set down his bucket and quickly surrounded James with a hearty embrace. After many pats on the back, hugs, and "how-good-it-is-to-see-yous" passed between them, Frank anxiously blurted out, "James, do you know that Elizabeth sold your farm? She's left with baby Charles on a wagon train. Do you know that?"

"Wha—what?" James struggled to comprehend. "They're not here? Is that what you're saying, Frank?"

Slowly responding, Frank said, "She's in the company of your mother and two younger brothers. They're far on their way across the plains to Oregon. They've been gone about three months now."

Plunging from his extreme high to the lowest low within a few seconds upon hearing this, James nearly collapsed. After traveling over fifteen thousand miles to greet his loved ones once again, he'd been expecting to clasp them to his heart within the hour. Instead, now he mentally processed that they were far away from here. They were journeying toward the setting sun to meet him. It was almost more than he could bear, and for a while he was completely stunned. The most he managed in response to Frank was moaning, "Nooo!"

He silently sank into Frank's arms. Frank led him into the house and placed him in a chair. Suddenly totally exhausted, James's want for food was long forgotten. Somehow he made it onto a cot provided for him and collapsed into a restless night's sleep in Frank and Helen's home. He had no memory of getting to that cot.

Giggling voices of young children near his face awakened him the next morning. He arose with a sudden surge of hope but soon cleared his head enough to realize that this wasn't his house, let alone his own family. Putting aside this fresh disappointment, he smiled and quickly rose to play with his little nephews. He immediately decided he was going to appreciate Frank and Helen's family while he could and set aside his personal despair for now. James appreciated their hospitality and genuine welcome, especially as he was just starting to accept that they were the only family he had left around here.

Soon, though, Helen corrected his thinking. "No, James. George is still here too. He helped the others pack up and leave, but he stayed behind to keep farming his own land."

For some reason, brother George had avoided the lure of the golden land out west and had stayed put. James wondered at this briefly, but mostly he was just very glad George was still here. At least he had a brother and sister to greet after his long trip away.

After James had collapsed in shock and exhaustion the night before, Frank had ridden over to tell George about James's return. So George rode over early that morning and surprised a waking James. James was just returning from the outhouse when he saw the horse and rider coming down the lane.

"James!" George shouted, leaping off his horse. He took several quick, firm strides and embraced his brother long and hard. Letting go and backing away, he said, "I'm sure surprised to see you back here. Mostly, though, I am so happy to see you're alive and well." He surprised James by grabbing him again and holding him for several more seconds.

Separated enough to talk finally, James nodded, "Yes, I am here, and I'm as well as possible. I'm just getting over the shock about my family leaving. I can hardly believe it still." He paused. "I may need to go look at the farm for myself to really get my head around the fact they actually aren't here. Frank told me that the Adams bought our farm, which is fine enough with me. Do you know if they've moved anyone into our cabin or not, George?"

George quickly filled him in on the doings of the neighbors who'd bought the farm from Elizabeth. He kept talking as Helen moved them inside to sit at the hearty breakfast table she'd fixed. Finally getting his appetite back, James ate like a starving man, which he'd been pretty close to on this part of his journey.

James knew everyone here was just as surprised by his return appearance as he was by the disappointing news regarding his family. He listened and tried to appreciate all of their local news. While they were catching up, James managed to keep his heartaches to himself.

Finally thinking of some good news to share, James cheerfully announced, "I ran into our William out in the California hills. We were both sure surprised to find ourselves on the same road going in the same direction out of Shasta City. We about didn't recognize each other, as he's looking a bit rougher and hairier than when we all last saw him. It was when he spoke that I knew it was him. He's doing fine and is well and strong. He loves it in California and has found enough gold to keep on mining there awhile longer. We spent six months mining together, until I needed to head back home, back here. He's made some friends with a few other miners, so it's my guess you probably won't see him back in Missouri."

Helen stopped feeding her youngest child, turned to James, and exclaimed, "I think that is just amazing, your running into him like that! What a nice surprise for you both. God must have brought your paths together. And how nice for all of us to know what he's doing now, too." She stood to start cleaning up their dishes just as George smiled and hit the table enthusiastically.

Heartily he declared, "That is truly good news. We haven't heard a word from him this whole time he's been gone. It's not been good, not knowing."

"Speaking of that," Helen broke in while reaching for their dishes, "everyone hoped to hear from you a long time ago,

James. When months went by without any news, it was very hard for Elizabeth and the rest of us. I know she sent off several letters with others going out to California after you left. Just before she left here she mailed another one to Oregon City."

James was totally dismayed to hear that both his letters and the journal notes he'd sent across the country to Elizabeth, along with hers she'd sent to him, never reached their mutual destinations. Frowning, he explained, "I wrote a lot of journal notes that I included in my letters, and I sent those off to Elizabeth at two different mail posts. I never dreamed they'd not make it back here." Then he asked, "George and Helen, if my letters ever do arrive, please keep them for me. I wrote out special notes about my trip that I really meant to share with my family. I'm so upset now to hear that they didn't arrive. I can still hope they'll make it here eventually."

It was right then that he gasped and blurted out, "Oh, no! I just realized that Elizabeth and the others will be equally disappointed not to find me out there waiting in Oregon. I've never thought of them until now—only my own disappointment. None of them will even know where to start looking for me. Who knows how long they'll keep wasting their time searching for me out there?"

James was overcome with panic. Would his younger brothers be able to care for Mother and for his wife and child too? He exclaimed out loud, "I have to get back out west! I need to get back there as soon as possible—hopefully before they do. There's nothing else to do but to return the very way I've just come."

Chapter 25

Elizabeth

After turning off from the Malheur River, the wagon train was forced to follow various streams. Eventually they left those streams to travel on higher ground to avoid multiple canyons in their way. On the higher route, they came to miles of dry, uneven desert. Their road was rocky, rough, and steep in most places.

After several days, there was excitement heard coming from up ahead. The word came passed along that they'd discovered some of the Meeks' wagon ruts from the previous year. Cheerfully, the front wagon drivers led them into Harney Valley, where Mr. Elliott chose their campsite along the Silvies River.

However, as they had been more than five days on the rocky and steep roads, some tired women began grumbling more and more every day. Jason confided to Mother and Elizabeth as they sat around the privacy of their campfire, "There's growing uneasiness among many of the men too. Some are having doubts regarding our guide. Mr. Elliott admitted to Captain yesterday that he's never actually taken this route himself. He'd come from the west to meet us using the Barlow Road, a more established trail. He knows his end of the new road back there in the valley, but this eastern part is still unfamiliar to him. I'm gathering that Elliott's only knowledge is from what others have told him. He has learned quite a bit from that guide Samuel Meek, too, who just brought a wagon train or two this way a year ago."

Jason went on to say, "The folks out in the valley where Elliott lives all claimed this is the best, most promising route. I know that Elliott is sincere. Though now, as the word is getting out that he's never actually taken this route, many are growing concerned. A lot of men—and even the captain—say they sense Mr. Elliott's lack of certainty more each day."

Mother Bushnell sighed. "Oh, dear. What you're saying is only going to cause the women to worry more. It's been quite obvious to all of us that this trail is getting harder and harder to follow. There's already been plenty complaining since noticing no signs or markers anywhere to be seen."

Elizabeth knew what Mother was talking about and chose not to add anything. That night while lying in their wagon and listening to the wind gusts hit the canvas, she prayed for God's guidance for them all and especially her brothers-in-law. She reasoned in her mind and heart that God saw exactly where they were and could move them in the right direction, regardless of the men in charge. She had to cling to that belief now and set her fears aside. Better yet, set her fears in the hands of that God who saw and knew all. After affirming that in her prayers, she slept soundly.

Despite these deepening concerns, they all still kept going warily along, forced to trust their guide. Two days following her believing prayer, a cheerful Mr. Elliott came down among the train announcing they were nearing some lakes called Harney and Malheur. It was nice to see he was actually right when they got close enough to see the first of these lakes. They'd reach Malheur Lake two days later, the captain said.

Two scouts were sent ahead to check out the water prospects. Those two rode back many hours later, dismally reporting that the lakes were full of alkali. They had not found good drinking water for people nor animals. Also they were alarmed at the number of Indians they'd encountered.

The anticipation over reaching water soon quickly turned to more discontented grumbling. The leaders were faced with more hard choices. In the end, they took Elliott's advice and turned east to go the long way around the lakes. They'd avoid the dangerous alkali and the Indians. Since this was going to cost them extra days of travel, tension set firmly in their group.

With optimism waning every day, it was hard for most emigrants to remain cheerful. Many were starting to get angry. It was impossible not to hear the curt and harsh words in neighboring wagons at night. Elizabeth developed a new appreciation for the Bushnell family, as they carried on optimistically without such anger. She'd been raised to believe that anger never did much good and mostly caused regret. *Where was these other emigrants' faith in the God of Providence?* she wondered. She'd noticed that at this point on the trail those with a true trust in God shined among the others. They shared and spoke kindnesses with a smile. She was thankful for the company of these more patient ones, and that included the McClure family. She had a growing respect for the even-tempered and cheerful captain and his sweet wife. Elizabeth and Mother spent any chance they could visiting and getting to know Caroline McClure.

Over the next several days, they traveled in mostly dry desert. The monotony in the landscape helped fuel the growing discouragement. After about four days into this desert detour, Elizabeth and others noticed their dry, dusty paths becoming much sandier. Soon after this, all their path became sand, surrounded by more sand. The trail was also turning darker. By midday, the wagon train found themselves among huge, soggy marshes. Within another few hours, all they could see around them was only this marshland. This abrupt change in terrain now caused greater stress and fear among the group.

Each wagon fought their wheels through the swampy, soft sand until finally the captain ordered everyone to turn around and head back again the way they'd come. All around them the Bushnells heard loud complaints as the order was passed down the train. As for Jason, Elizabeth, and Mother, they ignored the bad tempers and quietly accepted their reverse orders.

Instead of complaining, Elizabeth started singing to baby Charles, which helped her own spirits. He loved it and was completely undaunted by any uncertainties around him. The toddler's pleasurable chortles over her songs made all the Bushnells smile and brightened their spirits. Elizabeth was very thankful once again for this joy a child could bring into their lives.

After another day, now into their second week on the new trail, the wagons finally reached a large, dry clearing on some fairly firm land, and the captain ordered them to make camp there. Finishing their quiet, simple supper, the Bushnell family had just started to relax some. Soon, however, their rest turned into unrest as man after man started gathering between the Bushnell wagon and the neighboring Williams' wagon. The men were so nearby that Elizabeth and Mother could easily hear most of their voices. They heard many questions and objections.

"Can you tell which direction we went today?"

"What do those Indians mean to do to us?"

"Has Elliott even mentioned any good water coming up yet?"

"What did he say to the captain about having to come backward on our own trail today?"

There were lots of questions but very few answers to be heard. Mother and Elizabeth looked at each other intently. Finally Mother rose and gave a slight smile to Elizabeth; then she turned and began to prepare her bedding in the front of their wagon. Elizabeth smiled back and gave Mother a quick hug. Once again, Mother's sweet attitude was such a support to Elizabeth.

Elizabeth sat back down to continue her eavesdropping and watching little Charles being jiggled in Jason's arms. Jason and Cory both stood near the crowd of men edging around their camp. Deciding the brothers wouldn't be coming back soon, she began to pick up the coffee cups and started to rinse them. Suddenly she remembered their low water supply. They'd decided days ago to not wash the coffee cups anymore, but it was a hard habit to break.

As she stacked the cups on the wagon bench for the night, she started to think about her husband's trip a year earlier. *How would James respond to this upsetting scene if it had happened to his wagon train?* she wondered.

It then occurred to her that James's faith in God would help him through this type of situation. He was usually so good at trusting God in his life and not becoming discouraged. That he'd been so troubled over their farm in Missouri had been unusual; it was not like James to be so lacking in peace. That alone had made Elizabeth pay more attention to his talk and dreams about going out west.

Once she got her baby boy back from Jason and put to sleep, she crawled into her own bedding. She prayed over this growing distrust and anger among so many of the emigrants that night. She prayed and put her trust again in the heavenly Father, who knew exactly where they were and where they would head the next day. She was pretty sure she wasn't the only woman in their camp praying that night. Hopefully, all the menfolk would soon think to pray, too.

The next morning Mr. Elliott told the captain he'd heard about these huge marshes from Sam Meek's encounter the year before. He had hoped they'd traveled far enough south to have avoided them. Hearing that the marshes were familiar to previous wagon trains gave some a little more confidence in their guide—and some hope.

Mr. Elliott's attempt to lead their train while avoiding the stagnant marshes carried the McClure group farther to the south. Hopefully, it wouldn't be long before they were on the path to some fresh water and to that promised direct route to the Willamette Valley.

Chapter 26

James

Anxious to get back out west to find his family, James went back into Kirksville to resupply and get going. It was Joe, the stagecoach master, who informed James that he couldn't get back to New York in time. The ship had already turned back for the southern route. A steamer only sailed once a month from New York heading to South America, Joe told him.

Forced to stay nearly another month with Frank and Helen's family, James returned defeated. His time now dragged wearily along. His sister and brother-in-law were as good to him as anyone could be and understood his great disappointment. He was so close to what he'd longed for by coming home, but now so far away from what really made it home. He missed Elizabeth and their little Charles day and night now.

If he hadn't been so emotionally confused and physically exhausted, he might have started helping Frank and George around their farms with more enthusiasm. As it was, he farmed with his brothers out of no other choice than to pass the time while waiting to leave again. Soon enough, though, he found relief by getting into the rhythm of farm life, and he started to actually relax. James set about being useful by preparing and then maintaining George and Frank's equipment for their busy harvests. He cleaned, repaired, and oiled what he could. He took the things he couldn't fix into Kirksville, where Thomas, the blacksmith, could work on them.

While he worked, he got to talk with Frank and Helen about the previous winter and how discouraged most farmers had gotten. Frank had started building a gristmill on their creek in his attempt to alleviate their dependence on just farming. As they talked, James could hear the optimism in Helen and George's voices regarding their new plan. James helped work on the large, partially-built water wheel and was soon caught up in their excitement.

As he passed his time in Missouri, he was able to help with some of their harvesting before his stay ended. They brought in two of George's oat fields and Frank's potato field. A few of Frank and Helen's neighbors came over to help in exchange for some of the new potatoes. James enjoyed the fresh potatoes Helen fixed with dinner for about a week. Then it was time for him to start heading back to catch that next steamer out of New York.

With his few belongings packed, including some fresh food and supplies, James said his goodbyes. It was an emotional departure, as each family member knew they'd very well never see each other again. Even with that, Helen, Frank, and George all understood James's eagerness to leave and be on his way to Oregon. Unspoken were the questions of how their departed family had survived the trip and if James would find them safe and well. George had previously filled him in the best he knew of the Bushnells' plan. They would head for the reportedly best farmland, which was found in the mid-Willamette Valley. With all of these thoughts floating around in his mind, James finally got started on his return trip August 24, 1853.

He left St. Louis on August 27 by boat for Cincinnati. At

daylight the next morning, he watched from the upper deck as they passed the town of Cairo. Upon reaching Cincinnati, he went by rail through Columbus to Cleveland. From there, he traveled by boat on Lake Erie to Buffalo, then by rail directly to New York.

On September 4, 1853, from New York, James took passage on the *Georgia* bound for California. Even though his fare was $160, plus another $85 upon reaching Panama, he was relieved to be onboard an oceangoing ship again. He was quickly using up his gold, but his search for riches had been abruptly replaced by a more urgent search for his precious family now.

Chapter 27

It was the seventh of September, three days into his voyage south along the eastern coast. James stood among a few other brave passengers on the upper deck and watched the fierce wind. Then he suddenly heard the ship's sails being torn into shreds. With that frightening sound, all those close by him also realized how strong this wind had become. The next thing they all heard was deckhands yelling that the *Georgia* had sprung a fearful leak! Alarmed, James watched the crew head below and set about getting the pumps working. But the pumps were choked with coal and were therefore useless.

Soon there was eight feet of water in the hold covering the ship's coal supply, putting out the fires, and totally stopping the ship's engines. This now left them all at the mercy of the waves. The ship lay rolling in the trough of every wave, and many passengers feared each wave would send them to the bottom of the sea. The noises terrified James and his shipmates as they endured the ship's groaning and creaking in every joint. The cargo was loose and afloat in the holds and went from one side of the ship to the other with a thundering crash. It seemed the crates would soon break through the sides of the ship.

Amid the stormy darkness and danger, the passengers and crew—altogether some five hundred in number—roused to action. With the hope of saving themselves, they all went to work endeavoring to save the ship manually. Lines of men with buckets formed on every stairway. By tying ropes to the barrels, they bailed out water from the lower decks with a desperate hope of keeping the ship afloat until daylight.

Morning came at last and with it a slight abatement of the storm. As the waves subsided, some ingenious sailors managed to start the donkey engine and the pump by burning the ship's cabin doors. Amazed, James watched as door after door was jimmied loose and torn off. As other sailors hauled them down, he suddenly sensed a little hope within and grabbed one end of a door to help. With more rising hopes, James watched as the pump gradually began to win over the water.

After all the doors were gone, the captain yelled to the men, "Start burning the furniture next."

Every type and piece of wooden item was found and gathered to be burned. Voices among the crew became steadier and less frantic as the pump continued to lower the water level. Calm began to settle in among the passengers too.

All that day and into the twilight hours, James and many of the other men kept working at breaking up the piles of furniture and throwing them into the donkey engine. Shifts and teams were informally established to keep up a constant fire. As time went on, James began seriously wondering aloud, "Is our fuel going to last long enough to rid these flooded conditions?"

"Only time will tell, my lad," said the gray-headed crewman next to him.

As James feared, with the approaching darkness, the wood piles were almost consumed.

Even as he had worried aloud, some of the sailors were approaching the captain with a desperate idea. Apparently the captain agreed with them, and the startling order was given: "All men to start tearing up the upper deck flooring!" The news quickly spread down below to the deck where men were feeding fuel to the donkey engine. James and some others climbed up top to begin helping tear apart the tightly fit planks.

This was no easy task, as several years of numerous ocean waves had swollen and tightly packed the wood. Weary men began swinging the few axes still found on board. The loud cracks of splitting wood sent other men scurrying to their hands and knees and using anything they could find to pry up the broken boards. Others waiting close by grabbed the pieces and hauled them below. This demanding process required relieving the worn-out men as needed, but sailors, men, and a few women worked in grim determination taking their turns. Each felt it was in the hands of everyone aboard to keep the ship afloat and moving.

The next day these efforts succeeded in getting the water in the hold down far enough that a fire could be started in the engine room. The sweet sound of the main engine starting was like beautiful music reaching into downtrodden souls. Relief and hope finally stirred in James's heart—and probably all hearts aboard the limping ship. Greatest of all hopes, the ship was finally moving!

On Saturday, September 10, at 4:00 p.m., the *Georgia* and its passengers reached Norfolk, Virginia. As the ship neared the harbor and all danger was past, the crew, officers, and all the passengers assembled on the quarter deck. Their purpose was to give thanks to God for preserving their lives and bringing them safely to harbor. A bugler played two hymns that brought tears to many eyes, and a few wavering voices sang along.

Then, the captain spoke. "Because of the courage and wisdom of all you onboard the *Georgia*, and because of your willingness to help our crew, we are safely in port. I will always be grateful for each of your efforts and participation. As the commanding officer, I must praise my crew, who did such a remarkable job. I will always be thankful for their dedication and ingenious ideas that made the difference of life or death for all of us. I've asked Lieutenant Jameson to pray aloud the thanksgiving to God we are all feeling. Lieutenant Jameson, please."

James bowed his head with all the others, and they were led in prayer. It was a scene long to be remembered by the tired but grateful hearts in this group.

As most everyone predicted, the *Georgia* had sailed its last trip. It had to be replaced by a new ship that was back in New York. While they waited, all the passengers were put up in lodging near the wharf.

After a decent night's sleep, James struck out to look around this harbor town of Norfolk while waiting. It was a good-sized city. One of the most impressive sights was the unusual-looking Norfolk Academy. A proud townsman explained to James that it was a replica of the temple of Theseus in Athens, Greece. The academy was now a military academy, but it hadn't always been. It had undergone some changes of student body type over the past fifty years, but it still had the original buildings.

After that, James walked mostly around the wharf. He was delighted to find some coopers and watched them work making their barrels. James chatted with them about his own days making barrels on the Hannibal wharf. While visiting and observing them at work, he was surprised by the racial tensions he picked up between the white folks and the Negroes. He was glad to leave that behind and left there concerned that his own Americans could be so disagreeable to each other.

Three days later, every passenger boarded the *Crescent City*, the new ship that had arrived from New York. As they left port, James watched from the upper deck as the old ship stayed behind in port. Sailing away, he hoped never again to have another experience at sea like that one!

Chapter 28

Elizabeth

Three days later, the wagon train's small hopes diminished as they grew increasingly low on water. All of their provisions dwindled steadily too. The fears of running out of water and food were very hard to ignore. Now into their third week on the new trail now, they were looking at the same bleak desert landscape. It was still monotonous and dry, which caused constant murmurings and complaining among their neighbors. It was a serious day when the Bushnell women discussed being down to only a little flour and a handful of cornmeal. By the end of that third week, their water was also gone, and they ended up going on several long days without any at all.

Elizabeth guessed they'd been forced to go about seventy miles in this one stretch without any water. Praying often about this, she quietly just moved on each day. At least she could give baby Charles the cow's scant milk supply. But soon it too gave out. The poor cow dried up. All the Bushnells were so grateful for the cow's endurance and couldn't berate the animal. How much longer could any of their faithful stock survive?

One evening, when the travelers were completely fatigued and struggling into their fourth week, Captain McClure came to their camp and consulted with Jason. The captain said, "I want to send a party of some of the stronger men ahead to search for water. I've chosen you, Jason, as one of the three men. You're strong, and you also have a good head on you. Besides that, I've observed you have a good sense of direction. I believe, you, Charlie, and Jake will do a fine job scouting for us."

Jason agreed to the captain's plan and shared this with Elizabeth, Mother, and Cory that night at supper.

"Oh, Jason!" Mother Bushnell said. "Won't it be dangerous? You hardly know where you're going. No one does!"

Jason consoled his mother by replying, "Mother, we'll be able to move so much faster on horses without the wagons. We'll get to find water as fast as we can and bring some back. I'm sure it's not too much farther ahead." He added, "I feel it's my duty to the captain."

The women accepted that his mind was made up to go, and the family again prayed fervently that night, especially for the scouting party's success.

Early the next morning, most all of the nearby camps watched hopefully as the three scouts rode away in the northerly direction Mr. Elliott pointed out. That's where he thought they'd most likely reach water. The scouts were sent off with many encouraging words and best wishes.

Captain McClure instructed the rest of the group just to camp now and rest that day. Babies and children were let to play in the sand and dirt, a little food was fixed, and everyone tried to rest and relax with this unexpected break. Trying to straighten up things and rest was about all there was to do while waiting. Worry and thirst constantly fought hard for their attention too. A few men were attempting some repairs on their wagons, but they were obviously weak and they worked more slowly than usual. Elizabeth and Mother, and probably all the other women, really longed to do some laundry, but without any water, they just had to accept that everything would remain dirty awhile longer.

Eventually a few adults brought out instruments, and there was some music. But it was music to accompany their mood— slow and unlively. Nothing merry. Mother commented that it was a pleasant change, though, to be able to hear the lovely tunes. Even though everyone appreciated this chance to rest, the children were the only ones who seemed to really enjoy it. The adults were all just anxiously awaiting the return of the men and some possible good news.

Day one of waiting turned into day two. Then about noon-time, riders were spotted on the horizon. They soon proved to be their three scouts returning! Just the fast pace of their horses raised the hopes of all watching from the camp. Maybe they'd found water? The closer the horse riders came, the more en-couraged they were. Soon smiles and shouts of "Water ahead!" filled the camp. The scouts had found a big lake.

A smiling Jason rode straight to their wagon and dis-mounted. He gave his mother a big hug as she collapsed into his arms. "It's okay, Mother. I'm safe and happy to bring back a little water and the promise of more!"

Breaking their embrace and stepping back, Mother wiped her tears with her apron, saying, "I'm so happy to see you, son. It's been hard for me here just waiting and praying for your return."

Jason looked at Elizabeth, confused by Mother's tears. She reassured him that all was fine by returning his questioning look with a big smile and handing him baby Charles. "Here's someone who can't wait to get a hug from you, Jason!"

The toddler laughed delightedly as his uncle swung him in a

big circle, and that swing assured the Bushnells that all was well again—for the moment.

Each scout had taken buckskin bags, which they now carried full of water. Watchfully and carefully, the water bags were handed out and shared for drinking.

The captain decided to get the wagon train started again that same day and make some miles toward the northern lake. The wagon train turned northwest, and by the middle of the next day it arrived at what Mr. Elliott said must be Silver Lake. Mr. Elliott said confidently that he was sure there were more lakes soon to come. Despite Mr. Elliott's optimism, Elizabeth and the women collected water into everything possible just in case he happened to be wrong again.

Thankfully, they did reach another lake in the next two days. Elizabeth heard it was called Fossil Lake from Mrs. McClure. The captain's wife also said to the Bushnell women, "This means we're probably farther south than Elliott expected."

Not being exactly on the trail hardly mattered anymore to Elizabeth. Finding more water and getting a general sense of where they were and what direction they'd traveled eased her mind tremendously.

However, it wasn't long after leaving Fossil Lake the next day that they soon were back into endless dry desert surroundings again. At least now they had their water, but food supplies were still extremely low among all the camps. The next few days found Elizabeth and most of the women she knew struggling to stay optimistic. Elizabeth kept wondering what Fort Dalles would have been like and what supplies they could all have been enjoying by now. She decided those thoughts wouldn't help anyone and kept them to herself.

Mrs. Williams and her daughters complained to Elizabeth,

"Are we going to be stranded in the desert again? We can't go on but a few more days with the food we have. Why does the captain even listen to Elijah Elliott anymore? We'd do better without his advice, it seems to me."

Elizabeth tried to sound confident and hopeful as she replied, "I'm sure we'll be out of this desert area soon. I truly believe the Lord is going to get us all through this safely." She smiled as she realized she was speaking to herself as well.

Chapter 29

James

It was on September thirteenth that the *Crescent City* left Norfolk, Virginia, for Aspinwall, Panama. James greatly appreciated the smooth ocean voyage this time. On the nineteenth of September, the crew told the passengers that they were seeing Jamaica. As the ship passed that exotic land, many complained of the humidity and heat.

Arriving at Aspinwall on the twenty-second of September, James relished stepping on firm land again. Stretching his legs and looking around the small town, he found himself admiring this tropical, steamy, lush land. The Pacific Steamship Mail Company used the town as its main Central American port for the purpose of delivering mail to the American gold miners and settlers on the west coast. Learning this, he coveted anyone getting a letter over such a distance. He still had no news from Elizabeth or his mother. Even at that, he appreciated the mail service and the happy times provided for many others. He reckoned it wise of the US Congress to foresee this need just a year ago. It was an encouraging sign of progress that joined the two shores of his home country.

James's arrival now in Panama was timely. Thanks to Mr. William Aspinwall and some other associates, just in the past two years they'd built a new railroad here. The rail lines weren't complete, but would transport him almost to the other side of Panama. He couldn't begin to imagine, in his hurry to get back west, if he would've had to travel all the way around Cape Horn like many others before him. Going by train, he cut out weeks of further travel and all those added costs.

James boarded the polished, new railroad car the next day. The Panama Railroad was taking him as far as Barbacoas. The train's twenty-five-mile route passed through lush, tropical jungles at a pleasant speed. Sights and sounds of strange and beautiful birds entertained him, and he felt the breeze of the moving train temporarily sweep away his muggy, humid feeling. Inevitably, he and all of the passengers had to get out as they reached the village. It was the end of a very enjoyable ride.

There in Barbacoas, a few other travelers and James hired a small boat called a scow to help them up the Chagres River to Las Cruces. Their crew was composed of nearly naked natives. The scow moved slowly, as the natives had to pole or shove off from the shores many times. Once in the water, the small boat often had to be pulled over rapids and shallows. James hung firmly on to his seat and watched as these strange men carefully and silently worked the boat along. Mosquitoes were pestering all the riders, but the crew seemed to be able to ignore the pests well enough.

Finally the boat reached a small, native village composed of only a few huts. At this destination, the natives made several attempts at a tricky landing. The passengers were wishing they too had poles to help, but they were forced to anxiously sit by and watch the natives fight the current and eddies. They succeeded at last in landing after dark.

All were forced to spend the night there sleeping on the ground under the palm trees. Due to the warmth of the pleasant evening and plenty of experience at sleeping on the ground, this didn't worry James at all. However, once he lay down in his smooth patch among the tall grasses, he faced an unpredicted challenge. The insects were merciless! All night he tried to use his arms and travel bag in various positions to cover his head. In the morning, he still woke with more pesky bites than he could even begin to count.

Chapter 30

Elizabeth

Arguments broke out among the emigrants, even though Captain McClure and Mr. Elliott kept trying to calm their fears. Elizabeth hated the tension that filled the group once again. Jason, Cory, and Mother remained uncomplaining, but nevertheless they were still quieter than usual. Only baby Charles was able to laugh at everyday things, like the birds and the wind unexpectedly moving Elizabeth's bonnet strings. His simple pleasures and laughing made them all chuckle and helped them relax. Once again, Elizabeth was thankful for her child's presence and display of simple trust. She wanted to be able to trust like that too.

Late one morning the front party caught sight of what appeared to be groups of trees in the distance. Their news was passed down the train and hopes grew mile after mile as they approached that little oasis. Closer up, the trees seemed to be short and scrubby, but they were green. Jason, riding ahead, heard Mr. Elliott say, "Those trees are juniper pine, and they mean water is near!"

That comment was passed down through the wagons, but it wasn't exactly what the hungry women had been hoping for. Mother Bushnell wisely reminded those close enough to hear,

"Any water out here means animals come to drink here too. I think we'll get some game soon."

Trekking on, they came to those trees, and then more trees, and finally they saw another lake.

"I believe this is Summer Lake," Mr. Elliott said. "That means we have to travel north again to get back on track to the Middle Fork trail. That's where we'll head next, but it shouldn't be too far."

With this new lake and a landmark found, all their spirits lifted. A day's rest was declared at Summer Lake. The weary travelers watered their stock and filled up all their water containers. Then, as Mother had predicted, some of the men went out hunting. The others paused to enjoy the chance to clean and refresh themselves. The women discreetly washed themselves, hidden by the crop of junipers. But Cory and some of the men who'd stayed behind just jumped in the lake and bathed with their clothing on. Their laughter was reassuring to everyone. Clothes were washed and hung to dry, bedding and dishes were washed, and everyone relaxed. Cheerful voices could be heard around the camps again.

"Captain McClure and Mr. Elliott decided to send me and the other two scouts out again toward the north," Jason reported to his family. "Mr. Elliott thinks we're close to the new road, but McClure wants to be sure."

All Mother Bushnell replied was "Oh, dear"—to her credit.

The family somberly watched Jason ride off again early the next morning. At the end of the very next day—surprising most —the scouts rode back into camp. The scouts had already located the newly built road by its smoking ashes on their very first day. The fresh burns meant others had been recently working there. They'd followed the smoldering debris a quarter of a mile or so and then rushed back to report this encouraging news.

The emigrants had finally found their road! Enthusiastically, the campers all packed up and started traveling the following day. They reached the newly cut road and traveled it shortly before coming to an abrupt stop. Looking ahead of them, the road wasn't what anyone had anticipated.

Mr. Elliott exclaimed to Captain McClure, "This road was supposed to be cleared already. They promised me." Instead, the trees lay along the road where they had been felled but definitely not cleared. Mr. Elliott turned to the captain. "My neighbors and I all paid Dr. Alexander and his group to get this road done before fall. Apparently he's stalled coming from the valley end of the road. I just can't believe they stopped work," he said dejectedly.

Elizabeth couldn't help but feel sorry for the man. The emigrants had to admit that Mr. Elliott had finally gotten them to his new road. Then he—and all of them—encountered this upsetting disappointment. They were all feeling the same heartbreak.

Chapter 31

James

After taking some strange fruit and water offered by their crew, James and three others formed a small company and started off on foot for the city of Panama. Pointed in the right direction by the natives and using a compass, they left the village behind.

A good part of the way was over an old Spanish road. The road was paved with cobblestones, which were laid partway in the bed of a creek. The creek was at this time just barely filled with water. James was in a new pair of boots he'd bought in Norfolk, and they got soaked after all day of walking in this creek. His boots became so soft, he could scarcely put his feet on the ground. With each step, he miserably felt each stone underfoot. After an all-day tramp over marshy ground, he was hungry, footsore, and about as nearly done out as he'd ever been in all his life.

Arriving in Panama just after dark, they stayed there till the afternoon of the next day. Panama was a sleepy-looking old Spanish town built almost entirely of adobe brick. The inhabitants were composed of mostly mixed races. After a night of good rest and a chance for his boots to dry out some, James strolled through the town streets and along the old Spanish fortifications now nearly overgrown with trees and underbrush.

The greatest find that intrigued him was several old rusty cannons lying about in the underbrush.

While still exploring amongst these cannons, he heard the sound of the ship's whistle and quickly had to turn back to port. Surprisingly, it was already time to get aboard the next steamer, the *Oregon*. The ship's name seemed like a good omen. Climbing into a small steam-launch with a few other passengers, James was ferried to the ship about a half mile away. Once boarded on the large ship, he stood along the rail and grinned back at the shore. The closer San Francisco got meant Elizabeth and the baby were getting closer too!

Chapter 32

Elizabeth

Jason was wanted by Captain McClure. About ten men joined him in gathering around the McClure camp. They'd been called there to discuss the next action best for the wagon train.

Shortly, those men reported to their parts of the wagon company that they'd push on through the debris. The weary group prepared for the labor ahead.

As predicted by the looks of the clogged road, they moved along slowly. The men often had to stop and together move huge logs using the tired oxen to help them pull. In this manner, they gradually followed the blazed trees over the Cascade Mountains, sometimes only making a mile a day. As they steadily and laboriously worked through this road, early winter snows soon settled over the Cascades.

Even though it was only October and they'd worked just six days on the blocked road, the captain stopped the train. Gathering all the menfolk again, he declared, "We aren't going to make it much longer with our limited food and these freezing mountain temperatures. I want everyone to give me a report on how much food you still have after your supper tonight."

After their supper, the food situation was seriously discussed around the camp. The men gathered again to give their reports.

The captain made his decision. "I'm going to send Charles Clark, Robert Fandy, Jason Bushnell, Frank Owens, Andrew McClure, James McFarland, and the Olson brothers ahead in search of help. This group of eight men can get through on horseback where a wagon team cannot. They'll go ahead to try to locate settlers and alert them that a party is coming over the new road. The rest of us will move slowly on, hunting for plants and animals we can eat along the way."

Chapter 33

Morning came, and the rest of the wagon train all watched the scouts, led by Charles Clark and Robert Fandy, take off. Elizabeth heard quiet, tearful voices and loving words all around her as the families sent off the advance party. They were sent with six days' food rations. The Bushnells had prayed over Jason at breakfast, and Elizabeth had quietly hugged him in parting. For little Charles's sake, the Bushnells kept their goodbyes as happy as possible. Even Mother's voice was cheerful, if a little forced: "You will be in God's hands. Stay together, and don't take big risks—for my sake." She hugged him and smiled up at him.

Most of those also staying behind watched the eight horse riders struggle over the first log piles and a few big rocks. They kept watching until the men were out of sight. Elizabeth, with Charles in her arms, turned and kissed the little head, whispering, "Godspeed, Jason."

As the advance group pushed ahead, the rest of the train moved slowly. When they arrived at the Deschutes River in mid-October, Mr. Elliott thought they were on course again. He said they'd find this place on the Deschutes a good waiting spot. This river had been their goal when they'd turned toward what Elliott believed was the north. So when the first 150 wagons reached there, the emigrants were relieved to camp in this spot and wait for the other wagons to catch up. They were all hoping that outside help might find them here easily.

Most of the folks waiting took this time to repair wagons and tools and clean up again. The wheels were greased with what little fat or grease still could be found. The wagon axles and tongues were reinforced. Canvas wagon tops were stitched up and patched in any torn spots. Clothes, too, were mended. When the repairs that could be made were all done, some went about cleaning out their wagons of all the dust. When they were done with those chores, they rested. That became tedious too, and anxiety set in as they waited without much else left to do but cook a little and tend to their stock.

Voluntary prayer time was led by the captain every morning. Elizabeth and Mother attended this daily, and it was the highlight of Elizabeth's days in this waiting. Fervently praying that God would send help and return their men safely, Elizabeth felt peace and comfort and not the constant threat of worrying. Cory took Charles to care for the stock for any this early part of the day. He didn't ever seem to mind it, bless her younger brother-in-law!

While they waited, all were forced to watch their food supplies dwindle even more. The majority were very low on food. Men were sent out by Captain McClure each day to hunt for game. On a good hunt, the men only came back with a handful of grouse. Although any grouse was a coveted prize, it still seemed small, since it had to be shared around as many campfires as possible. Eventually some of the most destitute families killed some of their stock for food. It was sad to watch, but Elizabeth knew the sacrifice was driven by powerful necessity for those families.

The three Bushnells talked about butchering their cow but decided the animal was still too valuable for their future. The cow would help on the new farm once she was recovered and strong again. However, the smells of others butchering and roasting meat made their stomachs grumble terribly.

After five days camping and waiting by the Deschutes River, the captain decided he had to start the train going slowly again. As before, the route was littered with downed trees and rocks, which made their travel slow and arduous. In about five days of making less than ten miles, eventually some of their wagons had to be left at a big opening in the pine trees. In these cases, the oxen had finally just given out. Mr. Elliott said this was Hills Creek Dam, and maybe later in the spring thaw they could retrieve these belongings they were forced to leave. The train stopped and waited at this spot while a few of the unfortunate families made two-wheeled carts out of their wagons. Their cart could just roll along pulled by hand. A few carts were pulled by a solo remaining animal. Most of the other poor folks just put some of their belongings into others' hospitable wagons and resigned themselves to walking from there on. A few rode horses.

After starting off again and getting just about a mile farther, Elizabeth heard a sharp shout up ahead, and then the terrifying words, "Your wagon is tipping! Get out! Get out!" She watched the wagons up ahead all abruptly stop one after the other. The Bushnells stopped their wagon too.

"Cory, go help!" Mother shouted. She hadn't seen that Cory had already taken off running. He'd thrown the wagon reins down to Elizabeth in his stride. Knowing they needed to avoid adding more congestion near the accident, the Bushnell women anxiously waited back with their wagon. Elizabeth was very worried about the family whose wagon had turned over on this terrible trail. She remembered to pray for whomever it was.

Mother and she didn't have to wait long for the news to move along down the wagon train. Their neighbor reported, "The Johnsons' wagon tipped over and slid down the hill, along with their oxen. It slid right into the Williams' wagon. Several oxen are lamed, and Mabel Williams is stuck inside the wagon. She isn't talking or moving. They have to tip the Johnsons' wagon upright first. It'll take time to unload or shift a lot of items to get in to check on Mabel. It looks very serious."

Silence spread from wagon to wagon once the news reached each family and then was passed on. Elizabeth and the other mothers tended their children, trying to keep them quiet. Most of the men had gone ahead to try to help.

After more tedious minutes, they saw Cory walk slowly back to their wagon. "Mabel Williams has been killed in the accident. Everyone else was able to jump to safety or wasn't close enough to get hurt. At least two of the Williams' oxen are lame. Really it's a wonder that more weren't injured."

The train was halted for the rest of that day. Several of the men took to digging a grave alongside the trail. The shocked Johnson and Williams families were assisted in sorting and rearranging their disheveled wagons. The captain and other men were checking and mending wagon wheels and any other wagon parts that looked damaged. Several somber hours later, most of the train gathered as Captain McClure said a prayer over the fresh graveside. Elizabeth thought how peaceful Mabel looked as she was laid there in the dirt and stones. She looked over at the Williams children. The youngest two were being held or gripped by the other two children. Matthew Williams looked very pale and wide-eyed as he held and circled all his children near him.

Elizabeth couldn't imagine the loss he was feeling right now. She shut out that sight and squeezed her eyes closed as Aaron Adams played "Amazing Grace" on his fiddle and another very mournful song that Elizabeth didn't recognize. She tried not to think about how much she was missing James. She was trying to fight off her fear of losing him in a similar tragedy—or any other circumstance. That fear hung over her almost daily as the Bushnells traveled away from the Deschutes.

The next day they and all the others behind them struggled to get their wagons double-teamed and up the dangerous slope that had caused the fateful crash. It was near the end of that day when Elizabeth spoke to Mother about their little bit of corn-meal left. "Do you think I should get into it for dinner? We need to stretch it even more, and yet I don't know how."

Mother thought quietly and then solemnly said, "We can't. It's time for us to kill the cow. We just can't go on without some more food." Elizabeth started to protest but stopped herself. She quietly nodded her head. When the other families had butchered animals back at the last camp, they had held off. Now, trying not to worry, Elizabeth prayed that God would continue to provide for all their needs. If that meant their cow was going to provide them food, then so be it. Still, it was such a sad thought.

Upon hearing the women's gloomy food report, Cory quickly agreed to shoot their one remaining cow that same evening if the captain agreed to wait for the butchering. When the captain was asked, he assented to camp longer at the top of the slope they'd climbed. McClure also suggested that any other families who needed to butcher some of their stock do so here and now too.

It was a sobering time for them all. For the Bushnells, their one cow, White Star, had quit providing any milk weeks ago, but she was still considered a faithful part of their family. They knew quite well that all of the stock were an important part of their future in Oregon. Elizabeth grieved at this immediate loss and future loss for them, but kept her feelings quietly to herself. She knew they all felt the same. She patted the cow for the last time, holding little Charles up to have him say "bye-bye" to White Star. As she did that, she made the mistake of looking into the cow's big brown eyes and started to cry as the cow looked so lovingly back at her. A confused little Charles turned from the cow to his mother and patted Elizabeth comfortingly.

Jason took the skinny cow away from sight and shot it, despite the tears from the women. In the course of six hours, all the other designated animals in the camp were butchered. They created a bloody mess around the wagons that the wild birds loved. Elizabeth helped as much as she could, but keeping little Charles out of the way took most of her time. Soon, however, the smell of meat being butchered helped strengthen all their spirits. Elizabeth was suddenly cheered as she realized out loud, "Now we can share some of our meat with the other starving families."

She looked at Mother who nodded her agreement as she kept her hands busy with the butchering knife. Elizabeth thought for a bit and then listed off three families with many children to feed. "I think the Fandys, the Howards, and the Stewarts are probably the most in need. What do you think?"

Again, Mother agreed by nodding and said, "That would be nice." She smiled at Elizabeth encouragingly.

After the meat was stripped, deboned, and cut into pieces, Elizabeth and Mother cleaned off and then delivered some of the fresh chunks of beef to those chosen families, while Cory cleaned up their bloody work site. When the parents received the gift of their meat, gratefulness flowed from those three desperate families straight into Elizabeth's heart. Their deep thankfulness brought an unexpected and special joy to her. And so did the delicious smell and taste of meat that night!

No one took this gift for granted either. All three Bushnell adults knew some of their future security and potential livelihood had been sacrificed in order to sustain themselves and some of their friends on this trip. It was a sobering meal, but also very satisfying.

Then the clouds moved in during the night, and the downpour started.

Chapter 34

Elizabeth woke the next morning to a smell she'd come to hate. It was the wet canvas over her. Opening the canvas flap for some fresh air, she soon spied the wet mud around their wagon. That meant a day of trials as Charles fussed when she wouldn't let him down to toddle around in the mud. That added much stress for all around him too.

Mother and she resigned themselves to a wet morning campfire and then huddled in the wagon with cranky Charles as the train started to move again. Hours later, Elizabeth was exhausted from trying to entertain a youngster who wanted out to wiggle more than anything else. The wagons' slow movement in the mud was maddening, and they didn't get much farther that day or even the next.

Three slow weeks had passed since the scouts had left. For the last two weeks, the remaining emigrants had been forced to travel and camp huddled in or under their wagons, or choose to just get soaked. When they arrived a few miles above a creek, Mr. Elliott thought it was the Big Marsh Creek he'd heard about back in the valley. Even with this landmark found at last, they were too wet, cold, and tired to get very excited. Elizabeth heard children crying often, night and day, and she guessed that most of the adults felt like crying too.

On the following day, they were still in the Big Marsh area. The rain let up some, but not enough to get anything dried out. Most folks stretched and paced alongside the wagons, getting some heat from occasional sun breaks. The children got muddy but were much, much happier to finally be out of their wagons.

Halfway into that second day near Big Marsh Creek, food ran desperately low again. A halt was called and camp set up. Some of the stronger men went looking for anything edible they could find. Many had eaten unfamiliar greens found in the forests around and were now suffering stomach problems because of it. Mother, Cory, Charles, and Elizabeth survived on boiled cow parts and the broth.

For a second day it rained, but the rain was more inconsistent. They remained camped, and some men were told to go hunting for food. Cory joined that group. Just a couple of hours later, much earlier than she expected, Elizabeth saw him returning. She heard him holler as he approached. She eagerly watched Cory get closer. Elizabeth was just as surprised as anyone else in camp to see a bigger group of men breaking through the trees on the rough road behind Cory. First to come through the clearing was their most recently departed food hunters, and right behind them was the group of eight long-departed scouts! Amid all the cries of "The scouts have returned! They're all back!" and the joyous ruckus, Elizabeth suddenly realized that a very long pack train of strangers was still coming through the trees. Immediately she understood that their help had arrived. They were rescued!

Chapter 35

Elizabeth, with young Charles in her arms, ran to find Jason among all the newly arriving men. She got to him just as Cory and Mother rushed up on the other side to greet him. He gave long, grateful hugs to each of them and tousled little Charles's hair. He looked tired. Mother was quietly weeping, so he hugged her to his side and didn't let go as he started explaining.

"These strangers with us are settlers from the valley. When we finally ran into them, they immediately fed and sheltered us. Then, when they heard about us leaving you all starving back here over a month ago, they quickly got together food, supplies, and dry clothes from all their neighbors. It was amazing to watch all the local people there help pack up the mules and wagons so full within twenty-four hours. We left from the valley just yesterday with all this help. It still stirs my heart to see so much work and their generous aid," he said, his voice struggling with emotions and about to break.

The Bushnells all turned to watch the pack mules and wagons still coming through the woods. It was a truly amazing sight to behold.

Soon, Jason and a few of the other scouts were pulled away for a report to the captain. Elizabeth followed Jason though, not wanting him far away again. As they approached the McClures' camp, she heard Mr. Fandy saying, "We mistook the Three Sisters Mountains for Diamond Peak. At the time, we had no way of knowing we'd traveled too far north. We struggled across huge lava beds that were rougher than anything else we'd encountered so far. The lava cut our horses' feet—and ours if we weren't careful enough. After days crossing over the lava, you can't imagine how relieved we were to reach the McKenzie River. Then we just followed it down to the Willamette Valley. It was all harder and took much longer than we thought."

Another scout near him piped up, adding, "Near the end, all eight horses died. It was a sorrowful sight to bear, but we also needed to eat them. We'd been out of food by then for several days."

Jason said, "Following the river, we still spent several days crawling on our hands and knees through thickets, climbing over logs, and wading downstream. Our provisions entirely gave out again after the horse meat was gone. We ended up being reduced to necessarily eating snails, mice, and birds—anything we could lay our hands on. We didn't care anymore."

Their story went on. They'd finally reached a single man's cabin. The man took them in and cared for all of them immediately. This was where they'd learned about their mistakes on their route. The settler told them where they'd gone wrong, but they hardly cared anymore. They were beyond any interest but getting help for their families. As soon as this settler heard of the condition of the emigrants left behind, he got on his horse and spread the news.

"There wasn't a moment's delay as the neighboring settlers mounted an all-out relief effort. All that night, they worked in getting together supplies, and as soon as morning dawned, the large pack train was on its way for their relief. All these ninety-four pack animals and twenty-three loaded wagons were sent out to help the struggling emigrants," Mr. Fandy said with strong admiration and awe in his voice.

The newcomers shared that it was October 19, forty days since the scouts had left. That was big news to most of the wagon train, as they had lost track of time in their desperation. Elizabeth noted the date on the one piece of paper she and Mother kept tucked inside the wagon shelf. Such a day was to be remembered and celebrated! These rescuers had reached their desperate party waiting in the camp on Big Marsh Creek.

After spending the rest of that wonderful day getting nourished with delicious fresh food, getting into the provided dry clothes, and mending wagon parts again, the captain called for a time of praise around his campfire that night. Mother, Elizabeth, her brothers-in-law, and baby Charles all gladly participated. Elizabeth wasn't surprised to see that everyone else was there too. After the singing and giving of thanks aloud by many, some with tears flowing, the strangers and the McClure wagon train all lay down together around camp that night.

Elizabeth was certain she wasn't alone in continuing their thanksgiving for God's provision as she fell peacefully asleep in her bedding.

Chapter 36

James

The ship sailed for days within a few miles of the Central American shoreline. The air was soft and balmy, and the ocean, with scarcely a ripple on its surface, was clear, deep and transparent. Here and there James would see an immense marine turtle sunning lazily on the surface. As the ship approached more closely, the turtle would raise up its flippers, as if saying goodbye, and sink away into the depths of the ocean out of sight. From the ship, James thought a thousand miles of the country appeared to be mountainous and heavily timbered all the way down to the shores.

Onboard, though, life was not entirely smooth. One poor fellow had decided to work his passage up to San Francisco by doing the firing job in the hold down below. On their fifth day, James was on deck near enough to see this completely melted and burned man as he was brought up out of the fire holes. James and others around marveled that he was still alive. When James later looked down from the deck into these fiery holes forty feet below, they appeared like infernal regions. He watched the firemen down there, as black as night, shoveling the coal into the roaring furnaces and stirring up the fires.

The burned man died a short time later. This poor fellow was tied in a sheet and laid on a gang plank. A large lump of coal was tied to his feet, and he was run out over the side of the ship. Just as the sun dropped behind the western ocean, the impressive burial service for the dead was read by the captain. While the engines were stopped and everything was still as death, the plank was tilted. The body slipped feet first into the ocean and went down, down until it sank out of sight in the depths of the ocean, those dark mysterious depths. Then the engines were again started, and the body was left to the care of the wind and waters. This left James inexpressibly sorrowful. It seared a permanent and sobering image into his mind, and he knew the memory was going to haunt him for the rest of his life.

Chapter 37

Fifteen hundred miles north of Panama, the *Oregon* thankfully reached Acapulco, a beautiful Mexican town on a fine bay. Acapulco was a coaling station for the Panama Steamship Line. The ship anchored about one-quarter of a mile from shore and began taking on coal from the coaler ships lying in the bay awaiting their arrival. Most passengers, like James, were diverted by three to four dozen little Mexican imps. Looking to be between six to twelve years of age, the children swam cheerfully out to the ship. They lay about the steamship's water like a school of fish. James and others soon began to amuse themselves by throwing small silver coins into the water and watching the children dive after them. Amazingly, the children always caught the coins before they'd gone more than twenty-five or thirty feet below the surface! It didn't take the passengers long to figure out that these were very experienced divers who'd certainly played this game before.

James also watched in fascination as some cattle were brought out in a launch that moored alongside the ship. A rope was then thrown over each set of horns, and the cattle were drawn up by the head and landed safely onboard one after the other.

With fresh coal and the cattle loaded, they left port that same day.

The next day, after leaving Acapulco, some of the ship's machinery gave way. The *Oregon* was a side-wheeler with two paddle wheels. One of its paddle wheels stopped working. After the initial struggles and some attempts to correct the problem, the ship was obliged to run with one wheel the rest of the way to San Francisco. Thus slowed down, they arrived behind schedule on the twelfth of October. Being concerned about the delayed *Oregon*, another steamer was just about ready to leave in search of their overdue ship.

Upon disembarking, the passengers had traveled seventeen days from Panama, and James another twenty-three days from New York.

The SS *Columbia*, bound for Portland, had been held over awaiting their arrival. Under the tight circumstances, all of the passengers were herded right aboard the new ship and the next day were again on the ocean. It was on this final ship that James's heart grew more anxious. He was getting closer to Oregon. From his berth and also when overlooking the sea, he began to pray anxiously that God would be gracious to him again and help him quickly find Elizabeth and Charles.

The *Columbia* left the Pacific and turned east, moving up its namesake, the Columbia River. At the mouth of the Willamette River where it merged with the Columbia, the ship turned south toward Portland. Arriving just after dark on October 18, 1853, James had spent fifty-six days traveling after leaving his old home in Missouri for the second time. In just this round trip, since the first day of July, he had traveled 23,000 miles, almost equaling a trip around the globe.

Chapter 38

Elizabeth

It was easy to get up early the next morn and prepare to be led by men who knew where they were going! The wagons headed out northwest, back through the opening they'd broken through yesterday in the rescue. Those in the front of the train following the valley people began to see a small opening and a small valley that provided a passageway. Going through the rocks and cliff, Elizabeth stared and wondered at the passage, just as she thought the Israelites must have wondered as Moses led them dangerously through the Red Sea. The animals moved slowly and cautiously over the beginning of a crudely cut road and some slick rocks. However, animal and man had a new confidence that came with knowing they weren't wasting their efforts, as they were definitely going in the right direction.

At the end of the third day, Jason spoke to his family. "We'll be coming to some of the first settlers' homes in less than two more days."

Elizabeth and Mother smiled as young Cory cheered out loud, "Yippee! Hurray!" They all knew how he felt. Soon they'd sleep without fear of hunger or dangers and with hope of arriving at their final destination.

For the next few days, they traveled along more of the roughly chopped trail, but on the fourth day, there was a wider, grassier path that soon opened into a small valley. Elizabeth heard the men ahead say the valley was going to open up even larger just a few more miles ahead. Just beyond, she thought she saw a tree line that appeared to follow a river.

She called, "Jason, could that really be the mid-fork of the Willamette?" She hoped it was the river they'd all sought since parting with the other wagons over two months ago.

Jason replied, "I sure expect it's the very one," and they all smiled silly grins at each other. Cory soon got baby Charles to laugh, which made everyone laugh out loud hilariously.

On the following day, the wagon train came to the first farm. Mr. Briggs, who seemed to be in charge of the rescue party, started dispersing a few wagons to stay at each farm. The farmers were prepared to help the new emigrants until each family felt they could go on alone. As the rescued wagons approached each farm along their route, tearful goodbyes were said. Many promises were made of future reunions in this valley, their new home. Elizabeth hugged each of the Williams women and several others, saying, "We'll stay in touch. I've already learned to depend on the company of such good folks like you. We'll all need some encouragement from familiar faces as we start our new lives here."

Jason told Mother and Elizabeth privately as they walked on into the early afternoon, "Mr. Briggs plans on bringing our wagon and the McClures' to his own home site. That means we'll be the last. I've heard that he's got the biggest farm around and a successful lumber mill. I imagine we'll be glad to stay with them a spell."

The Bushnells watched more and more friends take off down the road and say their goodbyes. After another hour of following Mr. Briggs's wagon, they came to a grand looking home. Here, they were welcomed by Mrs. Briggs and were soon warming themselves around the fireplace. Elizabeth and Mother both exclaimed, "I can hardly believe we're sitting on real chairs!"

Then Elizabeth said, "I can't help but admire your lovely curtains and clean furniture. It's been so long for us. And to have china dishes and such lovely things around us—it is just hard to believe."

Mrs. Briggs smiled cheerfully and replied, "Oh, it wasn't so long ago that I don't remember what it was like to spend months on the trail. I just am so sorry you've had such a hard time these last few weeks. It must have been terribly frightening for you. I'm so happy you are finally here safe and sound."

They soon learned that the Briggs' parents and their uncle lived on the claims adjoining this one, as all of these relatives came to see and meet the bedraggled new settlers that evening. The Briggs' home had a room large enough for most everyone to gather, with children left to entertain themselves in the two bedrooms off of the gathering room.

The visitors were asked questions nonstop, especially about the news back in Missouri. Elizabeth found it very hard to realize that as long ago as she'd left Missouri, the valley people still considered their reports as "news."

Jason soon caught on that Mr. Briggs owned the town site they'd skirted as well as owning the lumber mill near the house. He reported that in an aside to his family and also said, "His uncle, Isaac Briggs, and Mr. Briggs's father are putting up a gristmill on the land above here, too. I see we definitely landed in with a prominent and well-respected family out in this new country."

When all the cleaning up and visiting was done, Elizabeth,

Mother, and the McClure women were sent to sleep. The women easily filled up the one spare bedroom and a few other open spaces in the house. The men gladly went back to sleep in the wagons. Since they'd allowed the women to sleep up in the wagons all of their traveling nights, they'd ended up always sleeping on the ground.

Cory said, "It'll be a treat to be off the ground for a change."

Chapter 39

By noon the next day, Jason and Cory were anxious to start exploring the area and begin looking for their own land claims. They left the rest of the family and the stock in care of the Briggs, and took off toward the south as suggested by Mr. Briggs. The women spent the next two days in the company of this pleasant and generous family. It took them a while to clean off the trail dirt from their bodies, clothing, and bedding. Mrs. Briggs was very comforting, knowing how she'd felt upon arriving only three years ahead of the newcomers. Of course, she had never been lost and starving, and she openly blamed their neighbor Mr. Elliott for his misguidance.

In the middle of the next day, Jason and Cory came back reporting, "There's plenty of good land awaiting us to the south! We've already staked two claims, marking all four corners the best we could manage. Based on what others told us, now we only have to go to Salem and get the paperwork done to make it official." They were grinning from ear to ear.

Mother Bushnell quickly put the damper on their mood. "You did all that without even consulting me? I thought I'd at least get to voice my opinion about my own land. Remember, I have been farming longer than both of you boys combined."

Clearly startled, the boys' grins quickly turned to surprised looks. Obviously, they didn't know what to say.

Elizabeth broke the awkward silence. "How far away is this claim? I think you should take Mother out there to see it tomorrow. That way she can see for herself what to make of it. Then you can head back up north to the office in Salem. I'm sure there's time still to be certain it's the right farm for all of you—before you two do any more planning."

Jason quickly agreed to her suggestion, and that broke the tension they were all feeling. Having decided to make the trip back to the property on the following day, they relaxed and described the meadows and timberlands they'd passed through. They described the Willamette River running from the east and then to their northwest. They had passed lakes and streams. Most hay fields had already been harvested, but they saw squash, pumpkins, and even some late corn still growing. Soon Elizabeth was caught up in their enthusiasm and decided she had to go with them tomorrow to see this new land, too.

Setting off from the Briggs place, Mother drove the wagon, with Elizabeth and baby Charles riding along. They followed the brothers along the dirt road and soon were in open fields of cut hay and autumn vines. They saw the two pristine lakes Cory pointed out, surrounded by cottonwood and willow trees that were almost bare of leaves. Several small streams rippled over rocks and moss making picturesque views in different places along the lane. At one point Charles gasped over a large crane taking off from the stream bank.

It was a delightful trip until they had to leave the lane and go cross-country over fields. The lurching of the wagon made Elizabeth hold on tightly to Charles, which he fought in protest. His complaining and the hard bumps and lurching made her ready to get out and walk, except they'd slow everyone else down so much.

Jason saw her discomfort and offered to take the youngster. He also assured her that it wasn't much longer as he swung little Charles up to ride horseback with him on his lap. That made the little one instantly happy—and his mother too. She was so grateful to have some family around for help like this when she needed it. She couldn't help but stop to wonder, how much longer would that be? How much longer would she be without her husband?

Jason pointed with his right arm and hollered, "The claim's starting over here." He got to some elderberry bushes that had a handkerchief tied to them and stopped. As they caught up with him, he continued, "From here to that creek bed lined by trees is one border. We followed the creek and on down to the next claim, which has been marked with a sign board. The settlers there told us this part was available and about how far we could figure it ran. This is what we think is the claim based on their word and advice. When we get to the landseer's in Salem, we can check it out on their maps."

He carefully passed little Charles to Elizabeth and then dismounted his horse. He walked directly in front of his mother and gently asked, "What part would you like to see, Mother?"

She turned her head and eyes from him toward the fields before them. She turned back and said, "Let's walk along the creek for a while. Then I'd like to cross over to that other side on the horse, and you can follow in the wagon if you wish." She was pointing to the east as she said "the other side." Elizabeth admired Mother Bushnell's ability to make her own decisions and watched as the boys both responded quickly.

It felt good to get down and walk, stretching her legs along the rough field of weeds and low growth. It was harder to get Charles's shorter legs through the roughness without him tumbling every few minutes. However, Charles was determined he didn't want to be carried.

Rather than forcing him to be carried by an adult, she let the others go on ahead of her.

"There's no hurry," Mother assured her. "I agree. Let him walk as long as he wants to."

Accepting that she and Charles would be going much slower, Elizabeth enjoyed the chance to look around her more carefully. At a toddler's pace, she noticed more interesting things—like ladybugs, small lizards that scurried away, and different birds singing from the grasses closer to the creek line. Slower meant colder, though, and she wrapped her woolen shawl over her shoulders more tightly.

She was relieved that Charles didn't protest when Uncle Cory drove the wagon up to them and asked them to have a ride. He let himself be lifted up and snuggled against Cory's chest. Thanking him, Elizabeth picked up her skirts and climbed in beside them.

Now they were going to catch up to the others, who were waiting where they'd turn to cross over to the eastern side of the plot. Once caught up, they all turned to cross the meadow. There were small, young trees along the way, some of which the wagon could run right over. Cory would warn the little boy, "Here comes a tree." He made a big deal about going over the trees. Charles laughed at his uncle and thought it was wonderful fun to see the tree pop up on the other side of the wagon. Cory did know when it was best to go around the slightly larger trees and several big rocks, which was a relief to

Elizabeth. She never knew for sure what these adventurous young men might try.

Approaching Mother and Jason on the eastern edge, she and Cory could see the other bandanna used to mark their claim. They'd used a dead branch stuck in the ground to make it visible. They each looked up and down an imaginary line heading north to south. Mother broke the silence and said, "I'm relieved not to see too many rocks in the soil. That will mean a much easier time farming here. Also, the creek is lovely. If you boys got the directions right, this is a very fine piece of land. I have a hard time believing it's been left this long unclaimed. You better go tomorrow to get it."

Jason and Cory grinned at her and at each other. Jason said, "Off we go tomorrow then! You heard her, Cory and Elizabeth."

The ride back seemed to go more quickly, and Charles actually fell asleep being rocked by the lurching wagon with Elizabeth's strong arms around him.

The next morning as she watched the brothers ride away to Salem, she seriously considered going to settle the new claim with the Bushnells. In many ways, she knew it was going to be hard to stay here with the Briggs when the others left her and baby Charles. She'd already agreed to stay here for a few months though, as that gave the family time to get a house built and settled in some first.

The Briggs enjoyed Elizabeth and the child's company. They had also convinced her to stay until James could be reached. That way Elizabeth and James could plot out their new life together. Convinced that was what the others wanted —and it made sense to her—Elizabeth had agreed to wait there.

She really hoped that James would find them more easily in this new, small town.

Chapter 40

It was with many mixed emotions that Elizabeth watched from the front porch as her family left without her for their new home sites. She had to trust God that this was the right and wisest thing to do, because her heart was very bound to those departing family members by now. She told herself, *Don't be silly! You can always go visit them soon.* She tossed her head, wiped her tears, and encouraged little Charles Alva to wave bye-bye. They waved until the Bushnell wagon and riders were out of sight.

Turning inside, she knew to be thankful that she was in the good and generous company of the Briggs. The next few days, Elizabeth tried to quickly settle into the routines of this family with whom they now lived. She found she could help watch the Briggs' children as she watched her own boy play and explore on his cute, little legs. She took to wiping up the dishes after every meal and learned where the cooking items were all kept. She swept the floor and picked up after all the children. The days settled into a nice routine.

When Sunday came, she was quite refreshed by going to a real church meeting. About seven families gathered there in the Briggs' big room for an hour of singing, prayer, listening to a Bible reading, and then discussing it. A potluck supper followed;

it was set up outside as they were enjoying a very pleasant late October day. It was here that Elizabeth met all the other families who'd helped her lost wagon train. She did her best to thank them all. She loved watching Charles play with all their children. At his young age, he mostly watched the bigger children and laughed at their antics. He tried to follow them around on his toddler legs, but they were much too fast for him. Eventually, a few little girls slowed down and took time to play with him. He was delighted and rewarded them with a chuckle, smiles, and a few of his own words that made the girls laugh. He was just learning to speak a few phrases, and they were funny to hear.

Now that they were here in the mid-Willamette Valley, all the Bushnells were inquiring about James and his wagon train anytime they'd meet someone new. One man had known James while mining in the southern Oregon area and had heard he'd left mining to find some other work. He'd heard James talk of getting enough money to go get his wife and child and bring them to start a new life out here in the valley. As exciting as it was to hear someone who'd seen James, Elizabeth started wondering silently if she'd been wrong to sell the farm and come out to find him. This country was so much bigger and emptier than she had imagined while back home. Finding James here was going to be harder than she'd ever thought it would be.

Then one day in early November, Jason and Mother rode over to tell her that they'd received news from brother William! He'd sent a message through a fellow miner to one of their neighbors. "He ran into James last fall," Jason said, "and the two brothers mined together the winter of 1852 to '53 near Shasta City, California. William last saw James in April. They'd parted their ways then so that William could go farther up the Sacramento River. He'd found a better vein and continued there still, but James had left William and headed alone for Shasta City. William thought James may have gone farther south from there, but he wasn't sure. He only knew James was hoping to hear from Elizabeth and wanted to return soon to Missouri and get her."

"Oh, no!" cried Elizabeth. "What am I supposed to do now? Did James go farther south still trying to strike it rich, or has he really gone home to find me? And I'm not there!" Her eyes filled with tears and her heart with doubtful despair.

Mother held her and said, "At least James was alive and healthy just six months ago. Just try to think about that for now."

It did encourage her that he was thinking about her and his family starting their future all together here. As she talked with Mother and Mrs. Briggs, the older women encouraged her to stay put and trust that James would find them. Unsure what else she could do, she took their advice and resigned herself to stay here.

She was dreading another long winter without her husband, though. How would he ever find them? There were no regular mail posts here, and they depended on word of mouth for most all of their news. She reasoned to herself that she must keep trusting that God, her heavenly Father, knew exactly where James was, and she could trust Him to get her family back to-gether again. Reunited! That thought comforted her and made her smile.

Chapter 41

James

Back in Portland, James was getting his bearings again in this rough, developing city. He saw and heard the familiar sawmill working loudly along the river. He noticed about a dozen steamship companies and a new-looking wharf. He continued his walk along busy Stark Street and passed a few trading houses and one log cabin hotel. James wondered why so many old tree stumps sat dangerously in the middle of the busy streets. The stumps had been whitewashed, and he watched townsfolk drive their wagons and buggies around them. It just didn't make sense to him. He had to watch where he stepped, too, as mud threatened to take over the wooden walkways in several places.

He saw there were still mostly men and very few women about town. James observed the few women around appeared to be of two types: the loose kind that would gladly help a man spend his money, and the others who looked respectable in their long skirts with modest bodices. These were the women who seemed to be helping their men make a living. James admired the latter and their adventuresome spirit to be making a home and family out here.

He found the stone-structured post office at First and Washington Streets and checked in with Postmaster Thomas Smith for any letters from home. There were none.

After enjoying this bustling city for a day, he knew it was time to start his search in the Willamette Valley. Boarding yet another steamship, he headed up the Willamette River toward Oregon City. Reaching the Willamette Falls, he got off below the roar and splendor of the unnavigable falls.

Upon his arrival, he was surprised that Oregon City had grown noticeably since he'd been there less than a year ago. His fellow steamship passengers, who were living here in their new homes, talked proudly of their incorporation as a city—the first and only official city west of the Rocky Mountains. "We've just become the center of the Territorial Government and have the first courthouse around here too," one passenger bragged to James.

Everyone needed to unload below the Willamette Falls. Those going farther south would have to portage around them. Once on shore, James began his amble through the town of Canemah into Oregon City proper. He could easily see about a hundred buildings in Oregon City, including shipyards, stores, mills, hotels, schools, churches, as well as a jail and a state government building.

The real aim of his walk around town, though, was to ask about any wagon trains that had recently arrived and to check the mail office for any letters from Elizabeth before it closed. James learned nothing encouraging. After several hours of asking many strangers and several shop owners, most of those steered him farther south down the valley. He gave in to their advice and started to plan his further travels.

The middle-aged postmaster seemed the most sympathetic of all and encouraged him to take the next steamboat heading south. This was the steamboat heading for Champoeg, as far south as any boat could take him.

Following that advice, James bought a ticket for the next day, as it was now evening. He walked to the south of the falls now where the ships going upriver were docked. He asked the busy ferryman on a nearby wharf about cheap lodging for the night. He was told to head for Mrs. Abernathy's Inn two blocks from the wharf, and he easily found the newly built and painted inn. There was a special price for sharing a room, and James was glad to take the cheaper option. He met his roommate, a Mr. Miller, who was traveling south also. They both dined at the downstairs table, and James enjoyed the fresh potatoes, carrots, corn, and baked chicken.

People here were friendly and interested in each other's traveling plans. One older woman was on her way to Salem to help at the Methodist mission there. Her tales of Christian growth among the Indians and churches for the new settlers very much encouraged James. He hoped there would be a church close to wherever he found Elizabeth.

Mr. Miller had started a freight warehouse in Champoeg and was in town doing banking business. James was glad to learn more about the next town in his journey. It had been picked as a prime spot for the Hudson's Bay Company and others to ship food crops and grains back to the developing cities along the Willamette.

The next morning, after a breakfast of boiled eggs and hearty wheat bread (the cheapest meal he could get), James was headed south on the Willamette River once again. Standing on deck so he could enjoy the river and fresh air, he watched the frogs splashing as they jumped ahead of the ship's bow and the birds taking off from their perches along the banks. He spied mostly cranes and hawks, but he also saw two bald eagles get their fishing spots disturbed. He enjoyed many other natural wildlife sightings along the Willamette, until they arrived at the Champoeg townsite about two hours later.

He and the dozen other passengers disembarked on the wooden landing. Most of his fellow passengers were home now, at their final destination. There were only two visitors among the group, including James. The other visitor was an older woman who'd already shared with him, "I'm finally going to get to see my new grandson and visit my daughter's family. They moved from our ranch near Fort Dalles over two years ago, and I have missed them every day." James was very happy for the woman, but also envied her excitement to soon get to see family again.

Looking and strolling around Champoeg, he saw close to a dozen house-lined streets but very few businesses. He spied a granary owned by the Hudson's Bay Company, a fairly new stagecoach station, and a big warehouse. Striding over to the stagecoach station, he seriously considered taking the next coach heading toward Salem. After getting the price, he hesitated due to his dwindling money. As the weather was pleasant and fair, he decided just to walk it. Besides, he figured he could search more thoroughly on foot.

When arriving at the four major roads converging in the center of Champoeg, he saw no signs and had to stop to consider which road he was to take. He watched a stagecoach come along behind him and take the middle right road, which James now thought must be the road to Salem. While still standing at the crossroads hesitantly, he was approached by a local fellow on his pony. The friendly young man confirmed that James was right.

James was off down that road with great hopes; soon he would hear something about his wife, child, mother, and brothers. As he walked the road that day, he asked anyone and everyone along the way about his family. He went as far as to share with some that he hadn't heard from any family since they'd left Missouri by wagon train in the spring. The responses were always very sympathetic, but unable to help him much.

In this manner, he made his way into the town of Salem within a few hours. Getting no news along the way, or there in Salem either, James reluctantly realized his search was going to take longer than he'd hoped. Almost out of money, he knew he needed to supply himself with provisions for a longer, further search. He'd noticed Salem was surrounded by fruit orchards. He thought maybe they were still harvesting some winter apples. He hoped so.

Hungry and discouraged, he determined to start asking around. Going to the nearest livery stable first, he inquired, "Is there anyone needing hired help around here?"

The man feeding the horses looked over and replied, "The last I heard, about a week ago, Charles Wilhoyt from up north was looking to hire some men."

James was astounded at the name mentioned and said, "I knew a Charles Wilhoyt coming across in the wagon train with me about a year ago. How long has this man lived here?"

"Well, he's settled north of here, and it was just a year ago that I first met him. It could be the same man!" the man replied enthusiastically.

James was amazed at his good fortune. Then he inquired about a cheap meal. The friendly man advised, "Go over to the stagecoach office, and the restaurant next to it has a 'traveler's special.' I hear it's pretty good."

"Well, that's me," James agreed. "Thanks for the tip."

Finding the café as described, James ordered the cheapest

item on the dinner menu: a cold sandwich and milk. Both tasted delicious to him. As he ate in solitude, James decided he needed to go see his friend Charles. After eating he went back to the livery stable and got directions to Wilhoyt's, which was about ten to fifteen miles north, up closer to Oregon City. Somewhat discouraged about the news of having to backtrack that far, he sighed involuntarily.

His new friend at the livery, Mr. John Mills, caught James's signs of impatience and spoke up. "You need to wait until tomorrow and start off fresh for Wilhoyt's. I can let you sleep here in the stable over there in the hay."

Going along with his new friend's advice, James spent a surprisingly comfortable night amongst the hay with a blanket and the warmth of the livestock. It was early when the animals' restless noises awoke him. James was glad to have an early start to his journey, though. While James was washing up in the water trough, Mills came in swinging his milk bucket. After greeting James, he set the bucket down and went back to get James a water canteen, bread, and hard-boiled eggs to keep him nourished on his trek.

James was deeply touched by this man's generosity. "Mills," he said, "I'll always remember your encouragement and kindness to me, and I hope to see you again someday. By then, I'm going to be able to introduce my family to you."

Mills smiled and replied, "I look forward to that day, Bushnell. I pray you find them soon. Please relay my warm greetings to Charles when you see him."

They shook hands firmly, and James was soon off, heading north again by foot. Traveling based on directions given to him by John Mills, he walked along a wide dirt road for several morning hours in the brisk sunshine. However, by close to noon, the sun was covered by dark clouds that threatened rain.

A white-haired and gray-bearded man came along behind him in a wagon loaded with lumber and offered him a ride. Gratefully James accepted and explained again where he was headed and the real reason he was on his travels—to find his family. The man spoke with a strong German accent and said he couldn't help James in that search, but he wished James well and gave him a ride as far as what he called "a colony" in the small community of Aurora. James learned that all of this colony were German immigrants who'd established their own religious community here.

Arriving at a group of about five small homes, the old man pointed uphill to the foundation for a very big house being built. They were expecting another group coming in the spring and wanted to get the big house ready by then. They would experience their communal living and everyone new would have a place to live upon arrival.

James took in all of this with interest. He appreciated that they were so strong in their religious beliefs and wondered how this community would survive over the years. He hoped to find out someday.

Before he could thank this devoted man and take his leave, an elderly woman came out to greet the two men.

Being introduced as Mrs. Keil, the old man's wife, both travelers got off and stretched arms and legs. Her German accent made it hard for James to understand what she was saying, but he understood her hospitality when he was given some water, bread, and apples to eat on the rest of his trip. Feelings of gratitude almost overwhelmed him as he weakly spoke his thankfulness, shook hands, and turned to take off by foot again.

After the restful wagon ride, he was able to walk briskly again. With relief he arrived at the Wilhoyt farm before dark. The first person he saw at the homestead was Charles himself.

"James Bushnell! What a great and happy surprise to see you again!" shouted Charles Wilhoyt. Lily Wilhoyt opened the rough-hewn front door and rushed out to greet him. She, too, remembered him from their wagon train and welcomed him graciously inside.

James told his story over a warm supper: his mining pursuits, his return trip to Missouri, his return trip west, and his search along the Willamette Valley. They were astonished at all that had happened to him.

"Someday, you need to add to your wagon train journal and write this all down, James," advised Mrs. Wilhoyt. "That is an amazing story."

"It'll be an even better story when he finds his wife and son," said Charles, and they all heartily agreed with that.

"We would love to have you work for us as long as you want, James," continued Wilhoyt. "Sounds like you need the work, and I need the help. Please make yourself at home here for as long as needed."

They lived on their land claim given by the United States government. Here James knew he'd experience his first time farming on some of the free land that had stirred so many to pack up and leave the east behind.

Starting work the next day, James was indeed impressed with the quality of this fertile land Charles and Lily had freely acquired. Working on their farm actually started him seriously hoping about farming this good land on his own. Once he mentioned aloud the idea of farming around this spot too, he was instantly surrounded by Charles's and the neighbors' enthusiastic encouragement. It wasn't more than two days before James selected his own piece of land, making plans to settle his family here.

However, in just another two days, his lonely heartache soon made him decide he couldn't stay yet. He was compelled to continue the search for his family. And so he turned down his chance to claim this attractive land. After a full week working with the Wilhoyts, he reckoned he had enough coins and supplies to leave toward Salem again. After thanking these generous friends profusely over and over, James optimistically departed from them—paid, resupplied, and encouraged.

Continuing down the valley, James was again in good hopes of soon finding some news about Elizabeth's wagon train. After visiting with some of the locals here, he was convinced his family's group must've come over on the new road going directly through to the Middle Fork of the Willamette River.

Entering once again what the Indians and some locals called Chemeketa, or what the American settlers had named Salem, James spent several days asking around. Diligently he inquired with as many locals as he could about that new route and any wagon trains that had come in on it. These inquiries forced him to spend more money than he'd wished on his lodging. It was on his third day that he ran into someone he knew—a fellow passenger from his San Francisco bound ship, the *Oregon*. Upon seeing him striding on the same boardwalk right toward him, James exclaimed "John Neely! It's so good to see a face I know."

Neely slapped James on the back in greeting. He said, "James, you look well! I'm glad you have filled in some since that slow-going sea adventure we had. I'll always remember how slow a ship goes with only one paddle. Won't you?"

He didn't really wait for James to reply but went right on to explain that he was just passing through Salem and heading on south to find his brother someplace along the upper Siuslaw River.

James said, "I'm heading for Springfield, having been told it was the only community with any road running from the east towards the Willamette's Middle Fork. That's where I'm going now."

John suggested, "Let's both head on south down the valley for a ways."

So, each welcoming the company of a friend, Neely and James left Salem together on foot within an hour. James's hope and confidence grew with their strides: surely that's where he'd finally find his family.

On November first, Neely paid for the two of them to stay at an inn just below the Bundy Bridge on the Long Tom River. The next morning they covered the short distance that got them above the village of Monroe. Due to their differing destinations, here it was that James had to leave the other's company. James was indebted to his friend in several ways, and as they parted, he said, "I'm filled with fear I'll never be able to find you again, John. I'm determined to repay you for last night's lodging. Where do you think you'll be in the next month?"

Neely just laughed off James's concern and said he was glad to help. Neely planned to stay with his brother along the Siuslaw or somewhere on the southern coast. Shaking hands and then grasping shoulders, they sincerely wished each other the best.

James said, "It will always be a comfort to see your familiar face, John. Please try to find me again around here, and I'll look for you whenever I get over toward the coastlands. I sure hope you find your brother doing well."

So once again, James struck out alone, afoot, and penniless. He was heading for Springfield.

Chapter 42

Leaving the Long Tom River behind, James crossed the flat, pathless prairie to the Willamette River. Mountains were outlining the prairie on both sides of the green fields. The land was completely flat for miles and miles. It was amazing to him that the fields around him were still so lush looking this late in the year.

In the next hour, he came across a farmer gleaning some remains of his late corn harvest. James stopped, and as they visited, this man, Mr. Bridge, told him, "This area, and for about the next eight miles, is the most southern point where any wagon trains heading to the Middle Fork would come through. A lot of new folks are coming through here every week, seems to me."

Increasingly excited to soon find or hear anything about his family, James thanked him. He struck upon the trail at the Bridges' place and kept going on it until he came to the Willamette River crossing. He finally had his turn to cross on the wooden ferry powered by a steam engine. He was truly impressed by such a modern ferry in these parts.

He got off in the small townsite of Eugene. The ferry master had previously advised him to head east of Eugene toward the smaller community of Springfield, knowing there were a lot of freshly arrived settlers in that area. The friendly man reported hearing that the population had doubled in Springfield since the arrival of the last wagon train there.

Nearing dark, James had to stop on his way to admire one of the most striking sunsets he'd ever seen. The flat land was silhouetted by western hills, and it was simply breathtaking as the sun lowered over them. He turned to the east and mused that one set of the darkened mountains over there resembled a horse saddle.

Starting up again after that refreshing pause, James soon came upon a well-managed farm with harvested fields that were already cleared for the next spring plantings. He followed the fence to a dirt lane and was soon looking at a handsomely timbered house with a newly painted fence running along its front. Hoping this would be the outskirts of Springfield, he stopped at the gate.

Before opening the gate and letting himself in, he hollered, "Hello! I'm new around here and need some directions."

A young man appeared quickly from around back of the house. Looking to be about fourteen or so, he strode up to James with confidence and asked, "What can I help you with, sir?"

Polite too, thought James. "Well, I've been walking all day from up out of Monroe and am in search of my lost family. I've been advised that a new wagon train arrived around here not so long ago. I'm hoping that my wife and child may have been a part of that." James removed his hat and wiped his brow with his arm in one movement.

The teen replied in a kind voice, "Come on in, and you can talk with my mother about it. There was a wagon train that got stranded a couple of weeks back, and the folks around here put together a successful rescue. We're the Harlow family, by the way."

James introduced himself as they walked up to the door of the house. The young man ushered him inside, and as James entered the whitewashed door, he glanced around at the comfortable and cheery room. The plump woman at the stove turned and looked at her son with questioning eyes. She quickly gave James a pleasant greeting.

James thanked her for letting him come in and gave her the same explanation he'd just given the lad.

Mrs. Harlow welcomed him to sit down and explained that this was their own free land claim they'd been farming for two years now. She explained, "You're about a mile and a half from Springfield, and you're right that a big group of new folks just got here. It was about two or three weeks ago. I know some of them, but I don't think I've heard the name Bushnell yet. But that group has spread out all around, so I sure haven't met them all."

Being able to tell how tired James was after his long day of tramping, she continued, "You need to eat supper with us. This is Sam, my son, and Mr. Harlow is still in town. We have plenty of food and a place for you to sleep right here."

So with her kind invitation, James settled in to spend the night with this hospitable family. He relished the warm meal she soon provided. Right after supper, Mrs. Harlow made a bed for him on their sitting room davenport.

James collapsed into this impromptu bed and had just fallen into a good sleep when Mr. Marlon Harlow came home from Springfield. All James remembered was this Mr. Harlow arousing him by shaking his shoulder. When James was awake enough, Mr. Harlow said, "There is indeed a young woman and child staying at Mr. Briggs' farm not far from here!"

Suddenly awake with excitement, James was now ready to take off again. However, he was reluctantly convinced by Mr. Harlow, who said he thought it was too late to pack up and go there immediately. Engulfed in a tumult of emotions, James was left alone and struggling to go back to sleep.

With such great anticipation, James really didn't sleep much that night, and neither did he stay for any breakfast the next morning. After he was dressed in the cleanest canvas pants he owned and his one untorn shirt on under his coat, he thanked Mr. and Mrs. Harlow. Sam was still asleep.

He began briskly walking in the direction that Mr. Harlow pointed out. After walking about two miles, he arrived at a very large white farmhouse with some impressive outbuildings around it. He was surprised at how well-established this place looked, with trees and flowers planted in a very pleasing effect. It got even prettier as he approached closer.

It was fairly early, with morning clouds not letting much light through. Slowing his stride, he suddenly paused to consider for the first time: Was it impolite to knock on a stranger's door this early in the morning? While pausing to think that over, he heard some noisy chickens in the small building about two hundred feet from the big house. Glancing over there, he saw a bundled-up toddler who seemed to be staring at the door to the chicken shed.

He cautiously walked over, stooped down, and asked "Hello. Do you need some help?" As the little one turned, it appeared to be a small boy under all those clothes. Then he asked the silent child, "What is your name, little one?" The young boy just stared up at him and then looked at the chicken shed again as if questioning what he should do about this man.

James wondered what he should do next, too.

Chapter 43

Elizabeth

It was a cloudy, late autumn morning, crisp and chilly. Elizabeth bundled up little Charles in warm clothes, a hat, and boots, and they set off hand in hand to feed the chickens for Mrs. Briggs. Breakfast was being made in the kitchen, but they always did this chore first. It helped keep the toddler out of the other family members' way, and they both enjoyed feeding the happy chickens. Charles Alva especially loved his daily task, and his little body shook with excitement at the first sight and sounds of the noisy hens. They neared the wire pen attached to the coop. Elizabeth enjoyed the daily chore too, as she was always caught up in Charles's delight.

She set Charles down as she unlatched the door to the chicken coop and told him to wait there as she checked inside and cleared a safe spot for her toddler to stand. Inside, she started shooing hens and the old rooster back up to their roosts. She needed to get to the feed boxes without chickens in her way and get Charles inside with her. That old rooster took his stance today and wouldn't budge, even for the food she held out. Not backing down, Elizabeth reached for the stick the Briggs kept leaning nearby for this reason and poked at the old rooster. He only moved an inch or two. *Oh, brother!* She didn't appreciate having to do daily battle with the king of the roost, but she continued to shoo loudly and poked at him once more.

She heard Charles start making sounds outside the slightly ajar door. They weren't his usual excited chicken feeding noises, either. *Hmm? That's not a good sign*, she thought, but she kept working to get all the chickens and the rooster up to their spots. Just as she'd finally poked that stubborn rooster onto his side of the coop, she heard a man talking to baby Charles. The voice didn't sound like Mr. Briggs or any of the men she knew around here.

Fear suddenly gripped her at the thought of her baby alone with a stranger. After she quickly stepped outside the pen with her eyes squinting in the brightness, she saw a man dressed in shabby work clothes stooped down talking with little Charles. This scruffy man stood up when he saw her appear. She froze mid-step at the door.

A desperate longing took over her. Could it be?

His height and stance looked like James. This man grinned directly at her. That settled it. It was her James!

"Oh!" was all she could manage to get out of her frozen throat. In a daze, she hurried down the ramp. Both quickly crossed the small yard, meeting with a long and hard embrace. Elizabeth feared she might collapse, but James held on tight to her.

When James finally released her and backed away, there were tears on both faces. Little Charles Alva started to wail. How dare his mother ignore him now for this stranger! Then, he couldn't understand why both adults just looked down at their distressed toddler and laughed loudly.

Smiling, Elizabeth picked up the crying child and hushed him while gesturing James to the porch steps. "We'd better sit down. I'm not sure how much more surprise I can take stand-ing up."

They moved, the three of them, and settled down to sit on the Briggs' porch steps. "Yes," said James. "I can understand what a shock this is to you. I don't have words to say what a relief it is to find the two of you. It's certainly taken longer to find you than I ever expected. I've been back to Kirksville, stayed a month with Helen and Frank. Saw George then too. Came back out west again on several ships."

"You've been to Missouri?" She sighed. "I feared that might happen. I wrote to you thinking the message would reach you. We took a wagon train out last spring. Then our train had plenty of troubles and big delays. Though we made it safely, it was because of the folks around here. They saved us. We were desperate before they came looking for us. Jason was on the scouting party that finally found the help for us. He's been truly brave. All your family has."

Elizabeth paused. "I can't wait to tell the others you're here! Jason, Cory, and Mother claimed their homesteads just a few miles away. They'll be so relieved to see you again. As you can tell, little Charles and I've been staying here, dependent on the hospitality of the Briggs family. It's been three weeks. We're joining your family once the men get the barn and a suitable cabin built for the winter. Maybe next month or so. At least, that was the plan." She smiled.

James chuckled in response and hugged her tighter. "I am so thankful that you and the others made it safely this far. I know some of the dangers and troubles of a wagon trip. Tim and I were blessed with health and strength for our journey. There were plenty of times we were protected from harm. For all of our safety, yours, and ours, I praise God."

Suddenly releasing her shoulders and turning to look at her, he continued, "Oh, Elizabeth! Another amazing thing is that I spent several months last winter with my brother William! He was still safe, healthy, and committed to mining in California when I left him. Running into him on a mining trail was a tremendous surprise. Only God could have arranged that. I feel truly blessed in many ways, especially now that I've found you, Elizabeth."

Elizabeth agreed. "Yes, we truly are, James. We all made it this far in one piece." She hugged her baby and her husband tighter. She also thought silently that James had a lot more explaining to do, but that could come later. For now she just wanted to sit like this on the front porch with their arms linked.

Elizabeth murmured, "They have some gorgeous sunsets out here."

"I noticed that." James smiled back.

Reunited after a separation of twenty months and crossing the continent four times between them both, now here they were, their little family finally all together in this new land.

THE END

Epilogue

After their dramatic reunion in the Oregon Territory, James and Elizabeth went on to homestead and farm near Clear Lake and then near Junction City, Oregon. James became a founder of many local institutions. He built and taught in the first school in that area. He continued serving on the school board after hiring new teachers to replace himself. When a series of floods hit the county, the farmers around him were left with no crops and no means to survive. James had wisely, and uncommonly, stored his harvested grains in his barn. He also had enough to share among his neighbors. This began a business that made him fairly wealthy: Junction City's first Seed and Feed Store.

James eventually owned several enterprises in downtown. He and C.W. Washburn started the Farmers and Merchants Bank where James remained president until his death. He also built and became President of The Junction City Hotel.

James helped found the First Christian Church of Clear Lake and then again the Church of Christ in Junction City. He was vice-president of the Oregon Christian Missionary Society and supporter of the Church of Christ Convention in Turner, Oregon, for many years.

James and Elizabeth had six children, of which only Lucy Janet lived into adulthood. After Elizabeth's death in 1868, three years later James married twice-widowed Sarah Page. Sarah brought two children into their marriage and they had four more together. However of those six new children three survived into adulthood. Sadly, James and both his wives suffered much loss.

Later in his life, James became concerned about the lack of ministers in the new churches of the Pacific Northwest. He personally paid for young preachers from the East to come out and fill the need. Then, he was instrumental in starting the Eugene Divinity School to meet this same need. He served as the school's President and then President Emeritus until he died in 1912. The school's first library was named the Bushnell Library and the school still houses a Rare Bible Collection purchased by James and his second wife, Sarah. Under the present name Northwest Christian University, the school currently has approximately 800 students.

A remarkable man with only a few years of formal education, James Addison Bushnell left his world a better place for many, many people.

About the Author

KATHLEEN PITNEY BOX grew up listening to family stories about pioneers and Native Americans. Traveling by wagon trains and stagecoach, relatives on both sides of her family settled in the Oregon Territory. Still living in the Pacific Northwest, she enjoys the beauty of the lands her ancestors discovered. While enjoying a career as an Elementary teacher, she delighted in teaching the history of Oregon Trail to fourth graders for 15 years in Vancouver, Washington. She developed a mock wagon train experience for her students in 1992 that still happens annually.

Being semi-retired has allowed Kathy to spend more time at their family built log cabin. Located in the Columbia River Gorge, where the first settlers floated by raft, she and her husband, Marq, their three adult children, and grandchildren all enjoy white-water rafting and hiking in the many of the same areas described in her great, great grandfather Bushnell's story.

CPSIA information can be obtained
at www.ICGtesting.com
Printed in the USA
BVHW070125140820
586229BV00003B/332